The Women's Press
science fiction

The Women's Press science fiction series features new titles by contemporary writers and reprints of classic works by well known authors. Our aim is to publish science fiction by women and about women; to present exciting and provocative feminist images of the future that will offer an alternative vision of science and technology, and challenge male domination of the science fiction tradition itself.

We hope that the series will encourage more women both to read and to write science fiction, and give the traditional science fiction readership a new and stimulating perspective.

JOSEPHINE SAXTON

Josephine Saxton was born in Halifax in 1935. She left school aged fifteen, was married twice, has four children and two grandchildren. Her works include *The Hieros Gamos of Sam and An Smith*, *Vector for Seven*, *Group Feast* a collection of stories under the title *The Power of Time* and many other stories in various anthologies over the years. *The Travails of Jane Saint and Other Stories* is forthcoming from The Women's Press in this series. She is now studying Traditional Chinese acupuncture and hopes to be qualified later this year.

JOSEPHINE SAXTON

QUEEN OF THE STATES

The Women's Press

sf

First published by The Women's Press Limited 1986
A member of the Namara Group
124 Shoreditch High Street, London E1 6JE

British Library Cataloguing in Publication Data

Saxton, Josephine
    Queen of the states.
    I. Title
    823'.914[F]   PR6069.A96

ISBN 0–7043–3992–7

Phototypeset by AKM Associates (UK) Ltd
Ajmal House, Hayes Road, Southall, London
Reproduced, printed and bound in Great Britain
by Hazell, Watson & Viney Ltd, Aylesbury, Bucks

For My Female Ancestors

The Antinomy of Pure Reason

First conflict of the transcendental ideas

Thesis
The World
has a beginning in time,
and is also limited in regard
to space

Antithesis
The World
has no beginning,
and no limits in space,
but is, in relation both to time and space,
infinite

Immanuel Kant
Critique of Pure Reason

1

Magdalen Hayward drove the car along a narrow road at a steady forty-five miles an hour. The way became more difficult as she went higher, towards the moors. To her left there were some remarkable rock formations standing out against the evening sky and she decided to explore them. She enjoyed scrambling over rocks. She gained a sense of freedom from being high up in barren country, alone. It was marvellous not to have people restricting, telling her what to do or not . . . but she would not even think of that.

She was not quite used to this car, the change between second and third was tricky, but considering the fact that she had not driven for a year, she was doing fine. She parked in a tiny lay-by and strode upwards through the heather.

The rocks were weird. Jagged teeth of the earth, half-buried monsters; people had carved in an eye or a few scales to define the illusions. The view from the top was magnificent. There was a small lake which did not look level but like a tilted mirror catching the last rays of the sun to dazzle or signal. Magdalen wandered around, taking an especial pleasure in the spongy peat and the fresh air. A blue butterfly flew towards her as if in curiosity, greeted her and disappeared.

She sat to rest facing the setting sun, her back against a rock. Wonderful place. She would stay and watch before she drove on, there was no hurry. She did not know where she was going yet and the question was not pressing. She was not expected anywhere, she could wait until choices appeared.

She looked more like a boy than a woman in her thirties. She was slender and wiry with long mousy hair, slightly crossed front teeth and a few freckles on her face. She had grey eyes with pale brown specks which people described as 'hazel'. She did not usually bother with make-up, and was one of those fortunate people who always look fresh and clean even on hot and dusty days. She thought she had better return to the car before dusk fell; it was possible to get stuck in bogs up here, and the path was rough.

Her jeans, white cotton shirt and sneakers felt like new clothes, though they were not.

It was wonderful to see the sun without a window between it and herself. It descended behind a distant coppice through air as clear as washed grapes. Everything was still, and after the last skylark, silent.

Magdalen rose stiffly, aware that she was not as fit as she would like. Too much time in bed was bad, and boredom slackened the muscles. She must look after herself, get herself toned up for her new life. Or her return to Clive.

Back in the car she smoked and then drove slowly down the winding road, thinking that perhaps a pub would appear which took overnight guests. But something went wrong with the car. The engine cut right out and she coasted along hearing the wind and taking more pleasure in that flying sensation than alarm at the problem. She checked the ignition, then stopped. Lights and wipers dead. A battery lead?

Under the bonnet it was too dark to see, and she did not know the design of this engine. Their own car she had been able to check in the dark once, to Clive's irritation. She sat on a low wall, smoking, thinking which would be best: to wait for someone to pass, or to set off walking. Then she became aware of the presence.

There was nothing to see at first but there was a high buzzing hum in the air. It came from the left which was the north, moving fast as she turned to look at it, low and glowing.

Elliptical, pearly and fiery, very beautiful. She felt paralysed as she tried to put up her hands to fend it off for as it came near

2

she could feel a prickly heat on her and her hair standing up wild.

The sound quietened and Magdalen fell to her knees with weakness, all her will had disappeared.

The sound stopped, and her consciousness waned as she was drawn upwards into the centre of the light.

2

Magdalen eventually realised that she was in a room without corners. Immediately she remembered her mother, who had always said of Magdalen's favourite aunt (ten years younger ten inches taller) that she should have lived in a house without corners, it would suit the standard of her housekeeping. A lifelong battle between the two sisters, one a perfect housekeeper, tough and tiny, one a scruff, daffy and tall, had influenced Magdalen. The mother would set her square jaw and remind Magdalen of Desperate Dan. The aunt would open her mouth and let forth a glorious mad laugh, but take Magdalen seriously when she said she wanted to be a famous painter. But even she had said that babies came from heaven.

'They don't make diamonds as big as bricks,' said her mother.

'But they put poison in little bottles,' said her aunt.

There was no dirt in this room. The air was neutral and pure. It should have been alarming, having no ceiling or floor or points of reference such as a door or lamp. There was light and warmth but nothing to see except the greyish walls.

A person could take a walk in a straight line for a hundred miles in this room; trying it out, Magdalen found that she did not fall from any surface nor feel the blood rush to her head as she traversed curves.

Wherever she was, that was the centre. So that was OK then. No point in trying to work out where she was, without points of reference. Something would happen eventually. The main question was why?

She sat down to ponder, gently scratching the material of the room. Some sort of plastic, but with a feel like animal skin, a bit like her own lips.

How big was the room? Hard to say but at a guess it was seven times her own height across its widest dimension; if she was her usual size that would make it about thirty-six feet. Too large. It seemed smaller than that. Not important.

She had come to consciousness here and could not recall the immediate preceding experience. Like waking up in hospital after an operation without the clash of bedpans and the click of nurses' heels. A silver dish across her throat to catch the spewed blood, age seven, tonsils and adenoids.

Strange, pale children queuing like pigs at a slaughterhouse, the surgeon blowing up rubber gloves to amuse and the nasty ginger boy shouting 'cowtits' and Magdalen the only one not laughing, but thinking, 'That boy's hair is like my Granma's chenille tablecloth!'

Then they called her name.

She sat upright expecting to wake but it didn't happen, and again her name.

'Magdalen.' Kind of electronic voice, moog effect, teevee SF.

'Hello?'

'Do not be frightened.'

'I'm not.'

'Good. Beings brought here are often in a state of terror, not necessary, we reassure.'

'Who else is here besides me?'

'None like you. You are the first of your kind from your planet.'

'Well it had to happen some time.'

'What do you mean?'

'That I would have a full scale hallucination of being captured by aliens. It figures.' She put down her Spode coffee cup, stubbed out her cigarette and looked her boring dinner guest straight in the eyes. 'Marcus darling that is just *too* science fiction for words!' Magdalen didn't take crap any more.

'We borrowed you to bring to our planet as a specimen of the

highest life form on your planet. You will be returned when we have noted everything about you, and you have nothing to fear.'
Wow!

She had scorned utterly all the flying saucer stories, having suffered a friend of Clive's for long hours on the subject, and even read magazines devoted entirely to the study of contact with aliens. She knew Jung's theory on flying saucers (yeah sure flying mandalas are a symbol of wholeness, big deal!) and had completely lost interest in the whole thing. Present experience rather than endless delving into theory was more important to her, she had decided, and Clive had seen her rebellion as a symptom of the times, rather than a personal need.

So if this was a delusion it did not matter; it was convincing enough to be real, therefore was real. No point in nipping her thigh to bring in some other reality, for who knew what was which?

'How come I am the first? I have read of many people being taken off to other planets as specimens.' As she spoke she remembered the light, the sound, the stalled car. Classic description in those idiotic mags.

'*We* have never been to your planet before. There are numerous worlds apart from ours. Your planet has not seemed interesting to us before, but we must fill in all records to attempt a total picture.'

'I see.'

'These people, they tell you what it is like on other worlds?'

'Oh yes. They say they are taken off to other places in a flying saucer and are interfered with on their wedding night and have their spinal fluids drained.'

'First question. What is a flying saucer?'

'A circular spaceship, glowing, with portholes.'

'Not ours. Very primitive. We transmit matter direct. Next question. What are spinal fluids?'

'Part of the material in our bone structure.'

'Thank you. Now, the question of looking after you. We have very little knowledge of your needs. We have brought a large quantity of your air to use while we manufacture more. It will be

6

helpful if you will describe what you need for life support and comfort. We can arrange anything within reason.' Well, looked at from some points of view she had met, that didn't leave much worth having!

'How kind you are. That *is* nice! Well. Tell me now, can you make *any*thing?' (Within reason.)

'Oh yes. Any thing. You name it, we have it.'

'How convenient. But I must know something. How do you manage to speak English so fluently? Almost colloquial.'

'What is English?'

'Our language. You are speaking to me in one of many earth languages and yet you know nothing of our culture.'

'The means of communication is simple. You are connected to our meaning transmitter in your room. Whatever we wish to communicate is translated in terms you understand readily. We find it interesting that your planet has more than one language, we thought one sample would be typical.'

'Not in many respects, but basically all humans are alike.' Magdalen was thinking that they had more or less told her that everything was coming from her own head, a suspicion she had been nurturing for some time. She simply heard 'them' speaking in English because meaning could automatically be translated into any set of symbols. What kind of device could do that? They must be very advanced. In science fiction novels, most other races were more advanced than our own even if they seemed only to be blobs of jelly. Did they mean her to tell them that for supper she needed protein, minerals and so on, or could they produce freshly grilled river trout with almonds? If they were very advanced it would not be a problem. With not a great deal of hope, she decided to try them out.

'Can I tell you what I would like for supper please? And I really need a bathroom and a bit of furniture, even cheap hotels have a clean bed.'

'Certainly. Just describe very clearly what you wish us to reproduce for you and from that and your clear vibrations we shall be able to rearrange things. But we must warn you that we can only reproduce things which already exist in the universe,

7

we cannot create totally new things, that is a different department and not for the individual need.'

'All right then. I think it would be a good idea if this was more
like a bed-sitting room with a small bathroom with – but do you
mean describe in detail? It would take a lot of time.'

'Please. What is time?'

'I don't know really. A measurement of the days, things going
by. How can you not know what time is? Everything is subject
to time.'

'We shall store these ideas and consider them. But you may be
reassured that your needs will be met. If you have a clear image
we can make it.' It would be like playing at magic. She had
wanted to do this all her life. Just close your eyes and wish and it
would appear. Real! There was still something in her which
wanted to believe that magic of that kind was possible. When
she had been in hospital to have her tonsils removed she had
tried and tried to make wish magic. She had been given a book
of *The Adventures of Rupert Bear* which she had found
enchanting. He had worn little check trousers and a scarf and
been very lovable. She had wished for him to come alive and
walk off the page so she could snuggle down in the lonely
hospital bed, cuddling him tight, talking with him. She had
wished and wished until she had gone into a blackness but she
had still fallen short of the requirements; Rupert remained on
the page.

Now, she wished for a comfortable bed in a room with
ordinary walls and floor, filling in details of Indian patterned
wallpaper and a blue carpet, drawers and cupboards with
clothes which suited and fitted her, cigarettes and an ashtray on
a table with a chair, a flowering cactus and a door. Dare she
open her eyes to check?

'Can I add or change anything after I have wished it?'

'Of course. But this process is not to be treated as a game. Our
intention is to keep you comfortable and in normal good health
during your stay with us. We have no intention of recreating an
entire world for you!' They were very perceptive. She had been
rather tempted to wish for something amazing like a huge

8

mansion full of wonderful furnishings, a swimming pool, a garden and . . . But of course, that was merely immature fantasy. Long ago she had wished to own a Greek island and entertain her friends upon it in great luxury, and who does not have such dreams?

She opened her eyes. It was a shock. Everything was exactly as she had requested but the carpet and wallpaper looked terrible together. She walked around the place, testing. Water in the taps, everything quite real and in working order. She approached the bed to test its softness, and there, sitting up and smiling, holding out his stubby arms, was Rupert Bear with his little dot eyes full of life.

She fainted.

3

She opened her flecked grey eyes knowing how they appeared because she had looked down upon them glimpsing their emptiness. They came to life.

She lay there thinking that she went in and out of states of consciousness as often as other people went through doors. This was not what she had intended for today . . . or yesterday? Time here was meaningless, she did not sense it passing. She had intended to drive away on an adventure, feeling her freedom, testing herself out instead of existing in the judgement of others, who said she was unfit to manage her own life. She sat up, and the room had no corners. Everything had gone. Oh dear, a delusion.

'What happened?' she called, not expecting a reply.

'We apologise sincerely for what happened. We had no way of knowing that the making of an environment would harm you. Please say if you know what will assist your rapid recovery.'

'Well, I could do with a glass of iced water,' she said, picturing it with its frost and tinkling. She had passed out at the sight of Rupert. He had been there, smiling and alive. Anyone would overreact to that. But, they had said that they could not reproduce anything which did not really exist. How delightful if there was a place where all the storybook characters really lived: Paddington, Zebedee, Fozzy, Pooh.

The glass of iced water was there beside her and as she sipped she felt full of new energy and stood up, spilling. The drops rolled off the stiff new denim.

'It was Rupert, the little bear. You said you could not reproduce things not in existence and of course . . .'

'We do not understand. We have no record of a thing called a bear.' Magdalen looked around at the nothingness as cool as her iced water. The Rupert had been as objectively real as anything else. She hadn't even said 'Hello Rupert'. That was very sad.

'But I saw him.'

'Sorry. No Rupert Bear.'

'But I saw him. Sitting in the bed.'

'We have just checked by attempting to make a Rupert Bear and it is not possible. A stuffed simulacrum is possible and this we did not do.' She had made a mistake. Hallucination. Amazingly convincing. She had occasionally had hallucinations when under severe strain. When her father had died and her baby had been sick and there had been no money to pay bills . . . But for heaven's sake, that was not herself, that was her friend Irma! She must try to keep things clear and straight, sometimes she identified so strongly with other people that it seemed she was them . . .

'I must have had an hallucination.'

'We are very interested. You are unique for a primitive being, most cannot reproduce things in any way. Perhaps you can make your own supper?' Did she detect a hint of the hope for economy in that voice? She could not have hallucinations at will, nor could she eat an hallucinated trout.

'I can't. It isn't in me. I don't have any power.' How true. No power at all. And it was what she had wanted, to let it all go, relinquish. To be a commoner, go around free, anonymous, to destroy the order, create anarchy by abdicating. She hadn't thought then of bringing toy bears to life, it was strange how plans turned out . . . she laughed a crack of rising cackle ending in a hoot and giggle.

'Please, what is that noise you are making?'

'Laughter.' Didn't they have that? 'I do that at funny things.'

'What is funny?' Lots of things.

'It was a passing thought.'

11

'How interesting. You are full of new concepts. Please continue manifesting and we shall create you a suitable environment once more. Shall we do the same as before?'

'No thanks. The curtains clashed with the carpet and . . . let's see, plain white walls, everything else a dark soft blue in different textures, restful and simple. After all, it will be temporary.' Won't it? How long would it take to find out everything about her? She didn't know a lot of it herself, probably. Certainly not all the biochemistry, a fascinating subject about which she had read a great deal. The pathways were so complex, and not all of them had been understood yet; Magdalen had early come to that conclusion. Which was only one good reason why it could be dangerous to swallow what the doctor ordered.

'We find it odd that you have more than one ideal environment. Perhaps you have more than one race in you?'

'I don't honestly think that changing the wallpaper has a lot to do with my genes.' And then again, it might have. They were noting down genes. Analysing them.

'A room isn't an environment. Well actually it is but . . .' Semantics was a real problem sometimes.

'The thing is, I just changed my mind that's all.'

'Changed your mind!' They were astonished at such a feat, as well they might be. It astonished her, when she thought about it; why was she not constant? How could external things matter so much? And yet they did, very much. In a room painted all orange, she would die.

'It is a phrase we use frequently, it means, new ideas occur frequently, deemed better than the previous idea. It is said that females change their minds more often than the male, but this may indicate only that they are more imaginative. It is said that a lady has a right to change her mind. But that refers to a bodily state in any case . . .' It was a bloody good job that she had never become a university lecturer, there would have been no way to sort out all the mental pathways associated with any single thought any more than there was a way to sort out a biochemical map, nor should there be for it was a matter of reaction, chemical or verbal chain . . . oh shut up Magdalen.

'We have a question. What are females and males?'

'Oh you *must* know that one. There are simply male and female made He them and all that, oh what utter bullshit, I mean I once read a book which stated that there were actually twelve sexes all varying degrees of male and female and then again there is the perfect balance of male and female which is an androgyne, said not to exist or only very rarely but male and female are two main classifications of human being, because our reproductive system requires that it must be so. That is one aspect of the matter, the other aspects such as maleness being the power to be superior without effort, thousands of years of conditioning having given them that, and so on are secondary. As far as a purely scientific consideration goes. That is.' Clive talked like that when explaining things, even in ordinary conversation he headed things 'A' and 'B'. She could see why now, it was because he didn't know what the hell he was talking about half the time but these mannerisms made it sound good or at least impressive but on the other hand . . . oh shut up Magdalen! Facts, stick to facts. What for example was the number of x and y chromosomes and why did a double helix resemble Ida and Pingala and why were not scientists interested in that?

'Yes. But we do not have a clear explanation of the male and female concept.' No more they did.

'It is not easy to explain. I once knew a middle-aged ex-army colonel, self-styled guru, who said that he believed that male and female were two species but I thought him wrong both then and now, because it remains fact that only the male and female of one species can breed. He was a crank and his mother had let him down badly which ended in him becoming impotent and selfish and neurotic, but he was like most other men in that secretly he not only hated but envied females. When you weigh it up he was justifying his own inadequacies, poor old bugger.'

'What is a bugger.'

'I used it incorrectly as a term of abuse. It is a man who uses the anal orifice for sexual intercourse, I could get specific but as you are having such difficulty with the concept of two sexes anything I say may be even more confusing.'

'We have sufficient with what you have said and all the concomitant mental picturing, thank you.'

Magdalen laughed aloud at the idea of horrible old Charles actually being a bugger. He was far too self-righteous to even think of himself in that respect, to enjoy himself at anything, let alone something not then approved of by the *Guardian*.

'Are you in need of food?' Magdalen forgot that her eyes had been closed, to think of food she opened them and found the room exactly as she had hoped. Much better than the patterns.

'Not half! I'm starving. I would really appreciate a lobster mayonnaise with endive salad, soufflé potatoes and some fresh fruit to follow plus a pot of good coffee – no not a pot, a cup of Turkish coffee with a bit of plain halva please. That would be great!' Wow! She had not eaten well for almost a year except for the few luxuries that faithful subjects occasionally smuggled in. They had been very kind and thoughtful but none of them had thought of, could not afford, lobster mayonnaise.

'And perhaps I could have a half bottle of Chablis rather cool, already opened. It would be a luxury you know but sometimes luxuries are necessities.'

Everything was there, laid on a clean white cloth, on plates. They weren't fooling, they got all the details from her mental picturing even to the girdle of parsley which she liked to eat, and a small dish of curled butter in iced water for the potatoes.

Magdalen got up and walked around, testing. There was no doubt that everything was real. She thanked her hosts and sat to table. There were two things she had not tested; the food, and the view from the window behind the curtains. Food was most important, she would need something in her stomach before taking a look outside.

'I am proving quite sensible in strange situations, I think I may have been misjudged,' she murmured to herself.

'Why don't you join me?' She asked them.

'Not possible. Thank you for the invitation. Don't mind us watching, we've eaten.' She didn't really like to be watched

14

eating; she wouldn't have to mind. She unfolded the beautiful napkin, heavy damask, and began her meal. Her first taste of the wine with the taste of the lobster made her spirits hit the ceiling. Not a problem to be watched, nothing could spoil this!

She was more than halfway through, helping herself to more endive (the dressing was just right) when she realised that this lobster was the best she had ever tasted. Always the idea of lobster was better than the actuality. Even the freshest from the best waters, cooked exactly right, had been less than her imagination. This lobster *was* the lobster of the imagination, and much more real than any from Cornwall or Massachusetts.

The flesh was thick and solid, neither soft nor tough, and so full of sea flavours that she felt to be drowning blissfully with every mouthful. The endive was like ragged taffeta in flames of eerie green.

The grapes and the nectarine were faultless. She felt it was all so good it was more than she deserved; she was not such a fool as to let this thought taint her immense good luck. She sat back then with her perfect Turkish coffee, the crumbs of cool halva melting on her tongue, the smoke from the cigarette soothing, and after a while went to lie on the bed, and there slept.

4

Dreaming, Magdalen drove along a narrow highway and stopped to look at some extraordinary rock formations. She was full of the setting sun, joyful and free. She dreamed that she was first captivated and then captive. The dream was a nightmare for then she was meat in a polythene bag, struggling to be free before the surrounding freezer made it impossible. Someone very large came to her rescue, ripping the polythene apart so that she could breathe.

'Do not be frightened,' said a loud voice, and she woke up looking into a face with a proboscis ending in a snout, three yellow eyes peering at her with great sympathy, and a tiny mouth much bigger than her own head. The creature stretched out a pale pad on an arm, one of many, and scooped her up to look more closely.

'So this is a human being. We want to know everything about you. Until then, you must stay with us.'

'Put me down you great loony,' shouted Magdalen unwisely. 'Do you not know who I am? I am the Queen of the States.'

'The Queen. How interesting. Tell me, what are the States?'

'It is a name given to America, the largest and most important place on my planet. I thought everyone knew that. The fact that I am English is irrelevant. In America, everyone is from somewhere else.'

'We know nothing about your planet really. But we want to know, for our collection of facts.'

'I command you to put me down at once.' She was turning over and over in space, infinite space.

5

Rocked violently, Magdalen awoke to find the bed in pieces beneath her and high laughter filling everything else. She felt terrible, as if she had been drinking, and then remembered that she had. The Chablis was her first alcohol in a year, and even so little and so good — but how could that make the bed fall apart? Reality was cracking at the seams again.

'Hoy! What's gone wrong with the bed you made?' she yelled, climbing out of a heap of broken wood and twanging springs. They had said they did not know what laughter was but they were certainly laughing.

'We are so sorry, ha ha ha. We wonder why you are not laughing ha ha. We have analysed your information on the subject and discovered that if we caused your bed to fall apart that would be funny. We find that to be objectively true. We now understand your concept "humour". We are splitting our sides ha ha ha.'

'It would seem that you have understood only a primitive form of humour so far. And that I have lost mine. The subject of a joke does not always laugh although I am beginning to see the sunny side of it, ha ha hee heeee!' She was laughing, but with difficulty. This had to be stopped or they would be putting salt in the sugar bowl, baking powder in the wash basin, her hairbrush in the bed.

'Why did you do it, was it an experiment?'

'Not really. We discovered that laughter is therapeutic and enjoyable, so we played a joke for your benefit.' Magdalen found this information touching. She felt a desire for closer contact.

'You know, I don't think I would be frightened if we met. I am fairly certain that I already know what you look like.'

'That cannot be. It might prove to be a great shock to you. Beings have become deranged from looking at us.'

'You can't shock me. I have seen such weird things. Come on, let's have a look.' Forays in the playground, I'll show you mine if you'll show me yours. Well, sooner or later it would come to that, if they wanted to know everything.

'We do not wish to antagonise you, perhaps we should describe ourselves first?'

'No need. I know. I'm sure you have a snout and three eyes and paddy paws.' Silence.

'And could you please fix my bed?' Silence, but when she looked round, the bed was made again, in every sense of the expression including the duvet shaken and replaced.

'Thanks. I may need to complete my sleep, I don't want my nerves to get shot.'

'Please, what are nerves?'

'Nerves are channels for impulses but in the way I used the word, I meant the state a person gets into through having too many adventures and too little sleep.'

'Most interesting. Well, we hope we shall not shoot your nerves. And now, please, how did you know of our appearance?'

'I dreamed you.'

'Please, what is "dreamed"?' Oh heck.

'I'm not absolutely certain. There are several theories current on my planet. I favour parts of more than one theory. I mean, I think the mind stores images all the time which come up in dreams as unused energy – for example I dreamed I was falling through infinite space when the bed had broken for example the image of falling I had seen in pictures I can see I'll never make myself clear because conversely or at the same time, I might have been falling through space in another dimension when the bed broke, sometimes dreams are very clear and then they feel significant, and some people train themselves to go into dreams consciously but look, it's all too much for me, I'm not a goddam lecturer.' She was tired and irritable.

'That does not explain how you could dream our appearance.'

'Not quite. I could have left my body and gone to take a look couldn't I? Could I?'

'We shall examine that question with all possible information. Leaving the body is something we do, but we had believed that only our particular life form did that.'

'And as you have no concept of time, that would explain how sometimes a person can dream the future, by which I mean, the dreamworld is timeless.'

'We shall enter your room, one individual.' After a short while Magdalen asked why they had not arrived.

'I am standing on your left hand.' A close examination showed a tiny insect.

'But you could not have spoken to me with that volume of voice, it isn't humanly possible!'

'I am not human.'

'You are very like I thought,' she told it. 'Except that in the dream you were many times my own size.'

'Ah well then, in the dream you must have shrunk.' It laughed.

'In dreams anything can happen, that is their advantage over normal states of consciousness. Whatever "normal" might mean.' She laughed. This must be a figment of her imagination for it spoke with her own inflections. And yet, perhaps that was the effect their 'translation' made, for they had only her own inflections to judge what her language meant.

'Normal must mean an average stage, we think. It is not possible of course from one sample to know if you are a "normal" woman or not.'

'Why did you call me "woman"? I don't believe I have used that word since I have been here?'

'We deduced the word of course. Do you find it insulting?' Well, that was a very good question. There had been so many times that it had been used as an insult that she could hardly separate the word from its usage. So often people called a man

19

an 'old woman' if they meant to be very cruel.

'If you don't mean it to be insulting then it isn't. It should be a descriptive word applying only to gender.'

'Which is how we used it. We have no reason to insult you and would be distressed to think you would return to your own world feeling that we discriminated on account of gender. To us, the idea seems insane.' She could certainly agree with that! Except of course, she herself discriminated on account of gender – she had to, because men were not to be trusted with certain things, unfortunately. But that was not the concern of her new friend sitting here on the back of her hand.

'Tell me, where is this planet in relation to earth?'

'Our modules for distance would mean nothing to you as indeed your module for "time" has no meaning to us. We have no time for such ideas ha ha ha!' This was a very subtle insect.

'Look, I hate to be a nuisance but I think I'm hungry again. I didn't have enough sleep and that gives me an appetite.'

'Yes. That is caused by hormone deprivation of a part of the amygdala in your lower brain.' Cripes! They had not been idle, and that was without taking off any spinal fluids at all. So many of those flying saucer books had harped on about spinal fluids she had half believed they might try something of the kind. The little creature nodded its head, a very human gesture.

'Just say what you would like.'

'I'd appreciate some toast with butter and French *chèvre* cheese, a sprig or so of watercress and a pot of Ceylon tea with lemon slices, please.' She sounded equable but felt irritable, a sign of low blood sugar.

The snack was on the table, in a shorter space of time than it took to make ordinary toast at home. What technical brilliance – might it be possible to learn some of their technology and transport it back to Earth? The toast smelled nice. Being very careful of the creature perched on her hand she went over to the table to eat.

As she reached out her hand to bring cheese and toast together she was suddenly transported back to when she was eighteen years old, but this time only in memory. Clad in black slacks, a bright green sweater, a herringbone tweed overcoat and string sandals on bare feet. Her hair piled high up into a large knot on top of her head. Elaborate home-made junky earrings, lots of make-up. An art student of that time. No state grant, no private means, therefore she was working her way through college as a chambermaid and as the life model at the college. She was having afternoon tea in the cafeteria of a department store on the way from one job to the other; she had been sitting naked with a draught to her back and an electric fire burning her shins, and had to face dressing up in a silly cap and apron in order to neaten beds and make sure that no commercial traveller had pissed in a chamberpot during the day.

At the college she had been told to pose naturally, so in order to try to get less of the sea fogs drifting round her shoulder she had subsided sitting forward into a shape like a prawn, and the art master had told her she was just like a Renoir or a Degas. She had almost wept at that for she knew it meant she was too fat. For comfort, she always turned to cafeteria tea and toast with a portion of Danish Blue. Her attaché case of paints and crayons stands on the floor beside her and she has a strong moment of *déjà vu*. A woman sitting opposite has put a bunch of chrysanthemums on the table and from them has jumped an insect which lands on her hand. Everything is crystal clear. She stares at the insect intently, she has seen nothing quite like it before. A snout, paddy legs, apparently but impossibly three eyes. Her curiosity overcomes her usual behaviour and she speaks to the woman at the table saying, 'Look at this, isn't it unusual?' The woman leans forward to see and shrieks.

'Good 'eavens, 'orrible thing, 'ere, let me get rid of it for you . . .' and sweeps it onto the floor with her glove.

'You silly old cow now it's lost . . . !' The woman stood up in a ferment, scarlet with rage. She gathered up her chrysanthemums and turned upon the girl and rebuked her loudly.

'You art students are abnormal, that's what I say!'

Magdalen had only one course of action. To leave the place herself, uneaten snack notwithstanding.

That night, after completing her evening stint as a chambermaid, she read a biography of Aleister Crowley which made her feel very sexy indeed and nourish ambitions to be a scarlet woman someday. Could the peculiar insect have been anything to do with Crowley's evocations? It was quite ridiculous, but she could not help feeling that in some way the two things were connected.

But she was busy designing theatre sets and sewing herself a new shirt in the following days, and forgot the whole thing . . . until now.

'I remember! The chrysanths in British Home Stores! It was you wasn't it?'

'I beg your pardon?' the creature said in a dignified manner.

'I mean, I have had what we call a *déjà vu* experience, I have been here before, or was then . . .'

'Perhaps you have just had a dream?' The voice was politely unbelieving, the archetypal voice of medical authority.

'*Déjà vu* is not a dream, it is a funny feeling you get during waking hours which always feels important. Some say it is just a trick of the brain cells, a sort of electrical fault which makes you experience the same thing twice or more – or feel you have done, but to my way of thinking that is putting the chicken before – I mean, that the electrical phenomenon is just the effect that can be recorded of having been somewhere before, and then again, in time.'

'According to your measurements and apprehensions, I myself live in a constant *déjà vu*.'

'That is a stunning possibility which I am afraid my brain cannot encompass fully. But it might get a bit clearer if I ate my toast and sent my blood sugar level up a bit. Toast is better hot.'

'Let me get you some more.' Magdalen saw nothing but when she picked up her toast it was uncomfortably hot to hold.

'Anyway, this time you didn't get swept onto the floor. Almost but not quite. That indicates progress.' The creature ignored her remarks and instead asked her if she would like anything else to eat.

'This is fine thanks, but I would like to go outside and explore soon.' A walk over the moors to blow away some cobwebs.

'I hope you will find it interesting but that cannot be yet; our atmosphere is entirely unsuitable to your physical system. We have constructed a protective suit for you but it is not yet thoroughly tested.'

'Well that's something to look forward to. Tell me, what is it like outside?'

'We do not believe that verbal descriptions are a good thing. Anything I could say would inevitably colour your eventual experience.' Oh sure. She felt tired rather than boosted by the snack, much as she had way back after the tea and toast indulgences. Then she had been obliged to work, now she could take a nap.

'Please do you think I could have my bed back?'

'Why certainly, and I shall leave you to rest.'

The creature disappeared, perhaps jumped or flew, and she retired to the newly made bed and curled up. She had expected to sleep immediately but this did not happen. The reason was that she admitted inadvertently to herself that she wished to escape. She felt a gathering threat in the situation that she believed even the most balanced person would not be so gross as to call paranoia. She was after all a prisoner. That implied the need to escape, it was inescapable. Oh dear – the puns again. She would repress it, she was fed up with picaresque semantic muddles, they led her everywhere. Which was all very well but not when she wanted to go somewhere in particular. She closed her eyes and began breathing rhythmically to induce calm. After a long while, she began to half dream while still awake.

She found that she could not move her limbs. It was a long time since she had been in this, the hypnagogic state. She did not try to fight it, for it might in fact aid her to find a way to escape. The trick was to relax and give in without sleeping. Although sleep seemed so attractive, this other state held more fascination – and might prove fruitful.

6

Magdalen chased away other hypnagogic images from the past, for they were all part of the same chain and linked themselves together like well-preserved sausages. A herd of bison on the lawn of the White House; she had barred all the doors and windows to keep them out. Although she loved bison they would ruin the carpets – and then through the only door she had overlooked had come a rhinoceros. Clive, playing analyst, had said it was undoubtedly a phallic symbol especially as it had pissed all over a red carpet, but Magdalen had said 'bullshit – Freudian bullshit' and looked for something more significant. She had never been scared of sex nor found it violating nor disgusting. Sometimes it could be very boring and clumsy but these thoughts she did not speak to Clive, who knew everything and was unshakeable in his pet theories. Then it came to Magdalen that here she had once more an opportunity to leave her body. It was not a real escape but it was better than nothing. Hardly knowing how she did it except that she did not make the major trip through the top of her head but simply slid sideways and parallel to herself, she got up and turned to look at herself lying upon the bed. She looked so peaceful, almost as if laid out for dead. 'Doesn't she look peaceful now, Mrs Thornton?'

'Eeeh yes luv, very peaceful. Gone to her rest at last poor soul.'

'No more pain.' No, and a lot less bullshit as well. Magdalen left the purely imaginary scene and went over to the window. Now was the time to see outside, for if it was too frightening she would inevitably return to her body with a big jolt and 'wake'. She drew back the curtains.

The view was fabulous. A great cliff of coloured lights in front of her, quite close to the window, alive, flashing on and off all over, hundreds of little coloured squares. Looking down she was on the very edge of space, a dark abyss out of which rose the lights. Above and away too, the limitless dark, with this vast wall illuminating everything before her. It was busy, alive. Millions of those little lights. An amazing pinball machine, a Piccadilly Circus or Times Square on a super-cosmic scale! She filled up with awe, physically affected, for the sight was unlike anything she had ever seen before, it was quite simply unearthly. The colours were far more vivid than stained glass or paint or light could be, she could not shut her mouth because of the strange beauty of the colours. She looked closer at one particular square. It did not flash on and off, it changed colour. They all did that, and then once in a while one would go completely black, become a fragment of the abyss below, then become a brilliant white and start into colours again. She tried to check if there was a constant or special sequence but could not keep up with the frequency. It certainly gave the impression of being designed rather than random, but Magdalen knew that the human mind desires patterns and will invent them, and delight in discovering them, for the feeling of security that pattern gives: the illusion of meaning.

The main thing was that it was all beautiful, wonderful and miraculous.

What was it? What sort of planet was it which could have a thing like that right outside the window? Where was the landscape, on what did the beings walk? Was there a flatness behind the cliff, was it like a massive billboard suspended in space? Was she at the top of a tower opposite a building? Like being in the restaurant opposite the Empire State building at night. No building could be that big. On a ship? It was no use trying to understand it, for if they had no concept of time that she could understand, it was probable that their concept of space was also incomprehensible. There were few things which could delight her spirit more than confrontation with the incomprehensible; it was this in her that had been the cause of so much trouble on many levels. It was a kind of curiosity without the questioning. Truly wonderful and incomprehensible mysteries were a great turn on, which was probably why human beings had needed to invent gods, especially God. Which went to show how shallow most people were, how little they were satisfied with, and how very easy to fob off and con.

Magdalen would have flown towards the miracle if she could for she felt it to be drawing her towards it as if it was really a part of herself. She put out her hand to touch the glass and it felt real. Her body was on the bed and yet this one came up against just the same problems – solid matter. That was definitely very odd – was she dreaming after all?

The vision was something like, no was, a computer. A massive brain, connecting circuits and messages. She felt compelled to go towards it and raised her fist; the glass smashed and the whole universe folded up and tumbled like a parcel of dirty linen into the abyss.

7

'We must not leave her unguarded if these crises come on so suddenly. It was quite unpredictable.' The voice had a note of self-justification.

'Oh yes indeed. Nobody could have forecast that she would do this.' The other voice had a note of both rebuke and self-righteousness.

'But she's fine now. Five pints I see. Temperature normal.' Magdalen opened her eyes and saw someone leave the room. Over her stood a nurse in a white cap held on with bobby pins, a blue and white striped uniform. Her fingernails were very long and painted silver. Her face was very cruel and she had an enormous bosom from which dangled a watch. Nurse Gerhard, German. A real bitch. Nurse Gerhard took a delight in making patients even more miserable than they already were. When Magdalen had been in the general admissions ward, Ethel in the bed opposite had been a victim of Nurse Gerhard. Poor Ethel.

Ethel, a woman in her seventies, rocking back and forth with some terrible guilt which could never be expiated. '. . . nobody knows the terrible thing I have done, I am beyond redemption, I am a terrible woman, a horrible nasty person, I can never never make things right again, nobody knows oh nobody knows . . .' and she would never tell anyone what she had done, it was too frightful for words, she would not tell even the psychiatrist. Everybody else got used to the woman after a while but not Nurse Gerhard. She used to bully her.

'Shut up you silly old woman or I shall have to punish you. I'll put you in a strait-jacket until tea time.' Ethel had stuffed the sheet into her mouth and moaned and mumbled through it, trying to be silent. Sometimes Nurse Gerhard would slap her bare bottom in front of everyone 'to teach her a lesson'. But no humiliation had any effect upon Ethel's grief.

'Ach, it is you!' she now snarled at Magdalen. 'What a silly woman you are, thinking you could escape your problems by cutting your wrist. The trouble with people like you is, they cannot face up to themselves!'

'I didn't do anything of the sort. I was just trying to . . .' She stopped dead. Caught off guard she had almost given away a secret which would be misconstrued.

'You see! You can't be honest with me! It is time you stopped behaving like a teenager. You think only of yourself all the time.'

'And of whom should I be thinking?'

'You should do something for other people, a woman like you without children should be able to do some good in the world.'

'Like you?'

'Now then, do not be so cheeky, it will get you nowhere.'

'Sod off you cow.' The nurse's face twisted itself into a mask of shock and hatred and then began to run at the edges into a mass of slime, and through the room blew a fresh wind with the scent of lilacs upon it, taking away the slow vestiges of her presence. Magdalen closed her eyes in relief, trying to glimpse again in her imagination the vision of coloured lights. It would not return, she had only a shade of it, a kind of *doppelgänger* vision which lacked authenticity.

'What happened?' she asked aloud.

'We saved you just in time. When you broke the window our alarm system warned us, and we came to give you your own air before you suffocated, and replace the window. We were very much afraid of losing your life but your minor wounds were easy to heal, fortunately.' How much better a cold scientific approach could be than a heavily emotional one – how comfortable, how clean.

28

'How do you feel now?'

'All right I suppose. A bit depressed. I need a change I think.'

'Or some food. That cheers you up. We have definite proof that your mood changes when you are very hungry.' That was true. Eat, sleep, wait, eat, sleep wait. Up and down up and down, trapped by a blood sugar chart for ever.

'What's on the menu?'

'Anything you desire.' Oh dear, they were going to make it difficult.

Until this moment she had been secretly and partly convinced that she was still in the mental hospital in her 'other' body, but being given a choice of food yet again destroyed that feeling. There they would certainly have given her no choice: thin meat, grey mashed spuds, gravy like dysentery shit and cabbage upon which some furious cook had worked out revenge. The worst food in the world. In that world.

She ordered smoked salmon, a lightly grilled lean steak, wholemeal bread and fresh goat's milk yoghourt with Jamaican banana honey; no alcohol, she needed all her brain cells! And before she got out of bed to go to the little table where the food was already set, she told herself to remember, all the time, that when she had begun this adventure she had made a bid for freedom.

Her aim had been to regain her own true rights and position in the world. So, to hell with negative impulses. The food made her glad to be alive. It at least was without fault.

Magdalen's senses were dazzled by the time she had swallowed her last spoonful of yoghourt and honey. Evidently the thick yoghourt had been the best Balkan, dark cream in colour and very ripe without being rotten. There had been exquisite fragments of beeswax in the honey, a refined detail which she had not requested or imagined.

Food fit for a queen. She was put in mind of the banquets she had held at the White House. The wild rice with grains separate and rare, the pheasant from her own estates, the sturgeon roe, the perfect Scottish beef. Even those feasts had not surpassed the food here; if they ever went in for catering in a big way then a six star marking would need to be invented.

She suddenly became aware that she was wiping her left palm nervously on the tablecloth because it was sweating profusely, and that her right palm was very dry and cold. This could be a symptom of repressed fear, or it could mean that her sun and moon breathing had automatically turned on. Magdalen was not unfamiliar with Tantric yoga; indeed, her husband Clive maintained that this was the cause of all her 'madness'. While Magdalen knew that she was not 'mad', she knew that she had opened channels within herself by fanatical overuse of certain exercises, and that sometimes these channels opened without her conscious direction.

But the image of the sadistic nurse had upset her because it symbolised something awful and evil for Magdalen; the perverted side of authority, the ignorant petty tyrant in a position of power. The Queen Mother and her teacher, her father and the Prince Consort – they had all been thus, and even when Magdalen had inherited the Crown she had still been under their power.

The nurse came into the room, solid and strong and sweeping aside all protest, efficient and full of mysterious purpose. She held a small measuring glass part filled with clear liquid.

'Your medicine.' Magdalen felt hypnotised. It was frightful stuff, that medicine. It was supposed to induce sleep but sometimes brought paralysed nightmares instead.

'Please take it away, I can sleep very well without that.' The nurse stood over her, one immaculate hand on one full hip, her legs planted firmly apart.

'Be a good girl and drink it down. Doctor says you must have it.' Which doctor? Magdalen giggled at the pun in her mind thereby weakening her position further. The glass was shoved under her nose. It smelled vile and caused a reaction.

'Do you not know who I am? You cannot order me about like that, and if I say I am not having that drug, then I am not having that drug!'

The nurse was not very impressed.

'Drink your medicine, it will stop your nonsense.'

'But I am the Queen of America! Begone! Sod off!'

The glass was touching her lips, spoiling her last words, two strong white knuckles gripped her nose and as Magdalen screamed the liquid was poured expertly down her throat. It burned and made her retch but it stayed down.

'You horrible bitch . . .' Her coughing took her over.

'Queen of America indeed! And she says she does not need medicine!' Laughing cruelly the nurse turned to march towards the door but Magdalen incensed leapt after her and grabbed the starched shirt as she slipped to the floor. The nurse screeching angry turned again to beat the patient about the face, dragging away, opening the door behind her as she hit Magdalen with the empty glass. Magdalen with pain in her cheekbone and the drug reaching her brain was limp but able to catch a glimpse of the incredible wall of lights before the door slammed shut.

'Let me come out please please I must get there!'

'Don't be silly, you aren't ready for that. Maybe you will never be ready, you are not fit!' There was the sound of a turned key and Magdalen lay dribbling saliva and feeling for blood on her numb face. Not much. What would they think of this? To them she was seeming always to die.

There were no dreams in the course of her very long sleep.

9

There was a dream trying to reach her through the barrier of the drug.

The world was a garden with several people in it none of whom she knew. They all loved her and wanted to be friends and they waited for her at a table under flowering lilacs. They were good people in a peaceful world. The waters in the garden were not poisoned and the air was pure, and everyone lived in harmony. They wished that Magdalen would arrive. One man sat apart from the others. He sat very quietly in a world of his own that was also part of the good world in which he sat. He too was waiting for Magdalen but he did not know that, he was only aware of a continual longing for something that he refused to name. He would know what it was when it happened.

He had an eccentric air about him and hid behind thick glasses and an ordinary hairstyle, but to a close observer he had beautiful large eyes and a sensual and generous mouth.

He held in his hand a single lilac floret and was meditating upon its centre. The gate to the garden opened and he looked up and Magdalen entered. He got up and ran towards her smiling like an idiot, tripping over tussocks of grass in his eagerness, but when he got close to his vision he saw that it was only a clump of peonies in full flower. He stood and wept.

Magdalen began to wake, and as she did so she dreamed a garden, but she had a dreadful headache and forgot the image including a sudden deluge of rain.

The coldness of that rain drenched her spirits though and her body was goosefleshed and pale. She wanted to go, to get out of things. But where was there to go?

Then the voice asked her what she would like for breakfast. She thought that she would be sick and did not answer but lay on the floor hating existence.

Existence. Hating it. When it was like this.

10

Jesu Christos! It was no fun being depressed. Magdalen had forgotten that she could be like this. It was so monotonous, always the bleeding same, when it arrived. Like the reincarnationist's memory of another life, recurring eternally round and round, the greater part of existence and no way to get karma.

When it passed it was put away like a bad dream and dirty linen, into the basket under the stairs to be taken out and washed some other day but not just now. There had been times when young that she had not known that she *was* depressed, when she had fondly imagined that she was merely being introspective. People had said, 'Mag, whatever's up, you look like thunder?' and she had always been taken by surprise by these queries not really kindly meant and answered, 'Just thinking.' Thinking was not quite the right word. She had often been recalling images and impressions very clearly; not exactly eidetically but at least photo-realistically complete with all senses; had she had an eidetic memory she would have passed the mathematics exam instead of falling in love with all the tutors. Tutors of all kinds had brought her unwittingly under their spell.

The colonel, her Gurdjieffian guru, for example. Out of his budgerigar chin he had stated that she had no buffers as other mortals had, that therefore her Kundalini flowed free where it would and she had replied that surely that was the point of Gurdjieffian work, to erode the buffers? Yes it was, but not so that the heart was destroyed by a white hot beam of pure love awakened at the least attention. Reverting to Freud, Magdalen had concluded that she suffered because she had not been breast fed, for were not females once babies too, in which case why were *they* not tit mad?

So what about the pain of existence? What utter rot, what bullshit she told herself, spitting mentally upon the Guru who, poor sod, had no comfort in him.

For what he had really wanted was her energy for himself, and an audience for his self-regarding poems.

The real problem was the aloneness in the universe. Anyone who thought that was not a problem was still dreaming. Especially being a queen, that only made it worse. Such a responsibility. Hard to bear and stay sane – but she had managed it, only of course at immense personal cost. And without the help of the royal physician who had advised skullcap, valerian and rosemary; rosemary was for remembrance – she had given him the sack.

Magdalen could remember everything from before the first shaft of light and the sound of the nurse answering her mother's query with the information that it was twenty to one.

'Came in at good odds then,' said her mother, drifting off into grateful nightsleep.

She remembered everything, even the exact colour of the base of a rose petal which fluttered onto the black rubber flooring of a bus on the way back from Haworth Parsonage one hot summer evening when she and two friends had got the giggles, a puberty blast of free Kundalini making all the passengers turn their heads to stare. The paintings of the Three Divine Sisters had caused that; the passionate evocation of another world, later to be borne off to museums but in those days in context, still full of the energies of their creators. And the rose petal had shone with an unearthly colour that had no name. The kind of rose petal which should have been combed out of the long red hair of some pre-Raphaelite heroine as she lay dying and thinking of Annie Besant's seven bodies within. Or without.

Magdalen suddenly sat up electrified by a brilliant idea.

'Hey you!'

'You called?' Just like the butler at the White House. You rang, Madam?

'Yes. You know you said you had access to information about me, based on my information plus your analyses? Well, there's something I'd like confirmation of please, and if anyone can do it you can. I wish you to investigate the reality of my multiple selves and the worlds which they inhabit. Can you do that?'

'Only if it does not entail harm to yourself. Our specimens must be returned intact.'

'I don't know about intact exactly. But do try.'

'OK. Sure.'

'Wonderful. And for breakfast I'd like a butty of home-made wholemeal bread with smoked bacon, Blue Mountain coffee with brandy, molasses sugar and thick cream, and a comprehensive selection of vitamin pills.'

'Madam, it is yours.'

By God, that was the way to deal with depressions!

11

She sat smoking happily after breakfast, musing upon the question of banning nicotine and legalising marijuana. Not a good idea, for whatever was prohibited was more popular. Better to let nature take its course for the nicotine, and urge legalising 'dope' to prevent criminals making money out of what was after all a very valuable herb. She hadn't taken any herself for a long time, but would someday – preferably in the right company. A twinge of isolated loneliness pulled in her chest but she breathed it out with the smoke.

'Magdalen, you requested an investigation.'

'Oh yes, that's right.' They were fast.

'We presume that you desire an objective truth.'

'From you, of course.'

'From our readings it would seem that a human being is incapable of realising an objective truth even when it is offered on a plate complete with parsley.' Well, she had to laugh.

'I think I know what you mean – but I wanted some chemistry and biology with regard to my concentric bodies you know – to me it's fact but other human beings tell me I'm deluded and crazy – I'd have liked some solid information to take back home to confront them with.'

'You really think anything we said would cut any ice?'

'Not really. Alas.'

'To minds constructed like yours a fact is not true until there is a vast consensus of opinion in agreement about the matter, we find. Conversely, it is not possible for us to refute your own

38

experiences. We observe that your experiences are objectively true. You have seven concentric selves, all interlocking, making forty-nine states of being, each with seven levels of intensity and each in contact with the forty-nine states plus contact with the original seven at all times and places, and a central consciousness which can freely move about to any point in this network at any one time. To us this is a very limited experience of consciousness but you seem to make the most of it, considering that you are not properly constructed, chemically speaking, for these journeys. We postulate that you are probably a sport of your species, and therefore not typical enough for our investigations.'

Damnation, just as she had suspected! Not a hope in hell of ever getting some hard and fast facts together that would make people see what was true, and make them leave her alone to get on with living. Ah well, that was life!

'Well, I'm very grateful. Does that mean I am to be rejected from your laboratory?'

'Not yet, if you will bear with us. We find you very interesting, and besides, many things about you probably are typical. We need a male specimen to get a more complete picture now that we have sorted out your sexual functioning.'

'Anyone in particular?'

'We have not decided. But first, we would like to observe you leave your body so that we can chart a precise chemical reaction.'

'I can't do it at will, I can never tell when it is likely to come on.' Silence. Well, it was true. She knew a few formulae but they didn't always work.

The nurse entered.

'I just thought I would pop in and see how you are. It's my day off but I still care about you.' She was dressed in pink jersey, soft high-heeled pink pumps, seamed nylons, silver fingernails, hair done by some pantomime make-up artist and she was smiling.

'How kind. I'm fine, thank you.'

'There now, I told you that medicine would do you good.'

'It wasn't that which did me good.' The nurse smiled cruelly, delighted to be crossed.

'I wonder when you are going to be sensible and admit who knows what is good for you. When people are ill they must allow themselves to be put in the hands of those who know better, isn't that so?'

'You are a figment of my imagination.' The nurse laughed.

'I thought you were feeling better.'

Magdalen called out to Them. 'Is she here or not? Tell me, is this nurse real or am I imagining her?'

'You are alone, the nurse is an unpleasant daydream.'

'There now you bitch, did you hear what they said?'

'I heard nothing, but obviously you are having auditory hallucinations. I shall go and report to the doctor at once.'

'Disappear, go, leave me!' screamed Magdalen. The nurse gave the patient a look of malice, turned and left, locking the door behind her.

Obviously, she had been a figment. Therefore there was no need to fear her again. Paper tiger, that was all. One had to learn to distinguish.

'Please could I have some fresh coffee?' She poured immediately while it was hot, savouring the fragrance. Scent was a vibration, but not as important as sound, stronger than thought. Here, she got her coffee if she spoke but not if she wished silently. It reminded her of a young friend who had flirted with the Divine Light and the Rajneesh gang, who spoke a lot about sound vibrations, mainly Om. The original sound in the beginning was the Word. Om om om om. In Gurdjieff they had danced singing oom-eem-aam-omm. It should have blown the top off your head but it had sounded like a Joyce Grenfell record of nursery music and movement.

She was restless and longing to explore outside. A walk on some moors for example. Perhaps if she imagined it strongly it could happen, like the Rupert Bear, for whom she had a sudden longing. She sat there concentrating, not doing very well. Time was passing, and she was aware of it. Slyly she asked them, 'Hey, I am experiencing time and yet you say that you do not have it. How come?'

'Time to us is non-existent. Time to you is existent. It fits OK. Where is the anomaly?'

It was a mind bender. She pondered upon it and got a headache, all thought of a wish-born moor lost.

'Just like you say. Where indeed?'

12

Clive Hayward managed rather well in the culinary arts considering the fact that until about a year ago he had hardly spread butter on his own bread. He had already learned to produce a delicious spaghetti sauce very similar to Magdalen's and had quickly mastered the tricky business of egg-and-breadcrumbing veal tournedos so that the crust was not greasy nor fell off in sheets. He garnished with parsley and lemon like an expert, twisting the slit slices into something like a topography model.

'You fussy bastard,' he muttered, seeing his feminine streak being well satisfied, even to three black olives. There was something missing. Of course, the thin slices of red pepper. None in the house! Tragedy! When he cooked for Magdalen he would not forget the red peppers, he would surprise her with having everything as perfect as she always had – but he was not cooking for her tonight. He checked that the caramel was holding up in the fridge, and then the table setting. Starched napkins in silver rings, a single rose by one plate, salt, butter curls, the lot. The doorbell rang. It was a large house so they had fixed bells everywhere. He clattered down the inlaid marble hall, skidding on the yak-hair rug, put it straight and opened the *fin de siècle* glass panelled inner door.

'Hello darling,' he said quietly just in case the neighbours had developed the ability to hear through fifty yards of shrubbery.

'Hello darling,' she answered with an awe that always had them fawning. She entered and he closed and locked both outer and inner doors and then took her in his arms in the veriest likelihood and similitude of a passionate embrace. The only thing missing was the real feeling, but perhaps that would start after dinner.

She trembled in his arms like a trapped dove, invisible feathers everywhere. He freed her and took her coat manfully by the collar which was a disaster as her buttons were still fastened all the way up to her throat and she began to choke. He had only meant to be polite. She undid the buttons laughing girlishly, red in the face, and he again took the coat and pulled at the hem of her sleeve intending to divest, but his foot slipped on the edge of the yak-hair rug again and he drifted sideways into the hallstand which rocked because it was top heavy with Magdalen's hat collection and he had to let go of the coat to steady the hallstand and a clothes brush intended for the removal of his dandruff unhooked itself from above the engraved glass mirror and fell on top of her head, which hurt for in its handle it had a circular wire loop which had rusted and broken and this actually pierced her scalp making it bleed. She discovered this fact when she rubbed her head spreading blood onto her ashen fair hair and onto her cream cotton gloves, and in horror Clive saw he had dropped her coat onto the rug which had loose hair which showed on everything except white which her coat was not. He bent to look at her wounded head but at that moment she lifted her head to glare at him accusingly and caught him sharply under the chin whereupon he bit his tongue which bled down his chin like Dracula dribbles, staining his teeth hideously when he grinned bravely.

Moira Cargill could tell that it was going to be yet another failure at sexual intercourse.

Clive led her into the bathroom and bathed her head and rinsed out his mouth with TCP, the scent of which Moira detested. His tongue hurt horribly.

'How farcical,' he ventured. She did not reply. He offered her a drink. She asked for a dry Cinzano. He got it for her, large, ice, lemon, everything – then remembered he had left the veal tournedos out either to go cold or be eaten by the neighbour's cat, or both.

They were intact but cool and soggy in appearance. He shoved them in the hot drawer and turned the potatoes over in melted butter, arranged the sliced beans, stirred up the salad dressing so fiercely it splattered his shirt front, an expensive raw silk which held stains forever, and rushed back into the drawing room to Moira who was making a good job of appearing relaxed on the chaise-longue. She was shivering. He turned on the gas fire.

Gratefully, smiling gently, she drew near to it. Gratefully, smiling meaningfully, he drew near to her. She shifted away.

'Dinner is just about ready darling, when you are.'

'How lovely.'

'I do hope it will be all right. I'm still not an expert cook.'

'If you said you were an expert cook I should be in trepidation for my digestion.' Moira played a lot of tennis, her calves bulged over strong ankles and one arm was noticeably thicker than the other, and to the acute observer which Clive was, one breast was higher slung. Her waist was tiny, hiding beneath a vast rib cage and curving hips. Clive realised quite suddenly as in a revelation that he did not desire her at all. Certainly he could never love her – where had that feeling all gone?

How could he tell her? After dinner? Over music – possibly the Four Seasons or Joni Mitchell? He was gripped with a twinge of shame like windpain at his unfaithfulness to Magdalen. It would go off if he ate soon. Always when she went away he had a mistress, or more than one mistress. He usually took about three months to realise that he could not live without a woman in his bed, and a further four weeks to realise that he wanted to sleep by himself and await his wife's return.

'Another drink?'

'Yes please darling.' She was very free with the terms of endearment. Perhaps it masked the fact that she did not love him either. Was it Louis Armstrong said, 'If you gotta ask, you ain't never gonna know'? It worked with telling love, too.

Not that she had any cause to be dissatisfied, she had an orgasm every time, if she wasn't faking. Perhaps she found him crashingly boring? He had been told that outright more than once. He made every effort to make himself interesting and attractive, the intellectual who is interested in what the other person has to say, teller of anecdotes but not stage centre all the time, a recounter of imaginary adventures and startling ideas. He had worked hard on all that, one had to these days. Perhaps he had worked too hard, lost the natural touch. Perhaps he had bored her pants off rather than ripped them off? He increasingly hoped so, it would be his access to peace and quiet, the right to sit for hours saying or doing nothing, arranging nothing. He held his second large whisky and ice like a grail, praying for that oasis, when he remembered the asparagus tips.

'Jesu Christos!' and flew out of the room, having another little game with the yak-hair rug which almost cost him six weeks in plaster.

Burned to a crisp, possibly a ruined pan. Moira mopped up the drink which he spilled all over her, wondering if he had got the shits again. He often got them, she put it down to nerves and guilt although possibly he lacked vitamin B. A very sensitive man but very boring in many ways. Academics couldn't help being boring, it was part of the job. She intended to initiate him into further gardens of delight with new positions for copulation. She had not quite got down to a definite plan for making him divorce his loony wife and marry her, but it was at the back of her mind.

Clive put the blackened pan under the cold tap which warped it. The kitchen was full of smoke. The veal was even soggier from its reheating but it could be served. He transferred the salad to the dining table and tossed the dressing over it, splashing his shirt again and the polished table. He peered mournfully down at his shirt, Liberty's, cost a fortune. It would scrub up into linty balls, he had observed this effect before with Thai silk. Clive laughed aloud at the phrase 'linty balls' and was rendered impotent at the thought of Moira's super-hygienic horror at his linty balls. He had to rush upstairs; he had an attack of the shits.

Eventually he was able to call her to table.

He poured a hock and she approved. They ate. He had

forgotten to wash his hands after the torrential bathroom episode and the germs spread from his hands to everything he touched. Also, the veal had been kept at just the correct temperature to make bacteria swarm joyfully in its juices. Moira ate greedily.

She thought of futures where she would not have much cooking to do, because Clive promised to be an excellent and enthusiastic cook. What with that, his house and money, and improved bed techniques, life would be wonderful. She explained to him however that his crème caramel should have a glassy shell around it rather than a runny sauce.

'How do you get it glassy then?' he peevishly enquired.

'I haven't a clue, I don't cook well.'

They took their coffee back into the drawing room which was now overheated. Moira removed her suit jacket. Clive loosened his collar, turned down the gas fire, and poured two apricot brandies to have with the coffee. He then put some Scarlatti on the deck, lowered the lights and put himself into an armchair, head back, eyes closed.

Eventually, without opening his eyes, he found and drank both his coffee and his liqueur. Moira watched him as he knew she would.

She watched tenderly, softened by the liqueur, contemplating a silent kiss on his forehead ennobled by a receding hairline. Dear Clive.

A huge piggy snore slubbered out from his lips.

For a second or so Moira was illuminated as to the cause of his wife's 'madness'. Greed extinguished the illumination but she still felt slighted.

At the end of the Scarlatti she left quietly, taking her coat from the hallstand without mishap and remembering to drop the latch on the outside door before she pulled it shut behind her. She waved and smiled at a female neighbour who just happened to be passing the gate with no outdoor coat even though the evening was chill.

'The weather is picking up,' said Moira.

'Warm for the time of year,' said the neighbour.

13

Magdalen visited Moira in her small modern flat, hanging her coat on the usual hook. It now seemed a long time since she had sought out and visited Moira with the intention of confronting her with breaking up her marriage. The interview had not gone as planned at all and they had become friends. Moira's own marriage was finished and they had appeared to be on the same merry-go-round of triangles, where each soul jostles to be supreme, eternally impossible.

'Come in and have a glass of plonk.' Moira sloshed out some Muscadet from a misted bottle and held out a dish of black olives.

'Have some of these, my deli has them from a barrel, they're Greek, quite the best I've had.'

'Some of the best I've had were Greek, too.' They both laughed. Sexist jokes were permissible in the privacy of your own home, but Magdalen recognised the defiant state in herself, of a quality which could tip the scales towards using men for pleasure and convenience. Why not? Because it stank was why. Their hands touched on the craft shop olive dish, and Magdalen thought, whatever became of my other dream, where I seduce Moira and confront Clive with it? I must have been at a very low point to think of anything like that. Wishing you were Lesbian was no good at all, you either were, or were not. Moira had lovers of both sexes, and had made a mild pass at Magdalen, which had almost reversed the dream except that Magdalen had felt embarrassed and idiotic. Moira had told her, 'Never mind, one day you will see the light I expect,' and Magdalen had replied, 'Yes, that would be great, I really wish I was like you sometimes. Only another woman could really *know*, I have often dreamed.'

'Darling I'm so happy,' Moira said.

'How nice for you,' Magdalen said, spitting out the very bitter Greek olive as politely as possible. 'What is the cause of this happiness? Has Clive remembered your anniversary or something?' Moira pealed out laughter.

'I'm in love again. A wonderful woman I met at the tennis club, she's half Portuguese. Look, I have a photo.' Magdalen looked and saw a sad and beautiful girl sitting on a wooden bench dressed in tennis whites.

'Lovely. You're very lucky.'

'I know. I think this is it.'

'And are you still seeing my ex?'

'Well yes, but he's got another girl as well you know, one of his students.'

'I am not at all surprised.' Or hurt, not like I used to be. What do I feel? Envy. Just a little envy is all, for I too need to love someone.

'I've brought back your Marge Piercy. I find her relentless.'

'Yes, that's what I like about her. Do you want your Iris Murdoch back?'

'If you've finished with it, it isn't important.'

'I haven't read it yet actually, it isn't quite my thing.'

'I can't put them down once I've started, it's a vice like Mars bars are with some people.'

'Or those women who read Mills and Boon.' Magdalen's heart felt physical pain at the sudden feeling of being a woman who had so little in her life that she was addicted to Romance. She imagined the pink silk coverlet, the chocolates, the glasses on a chain around the neck, the frilled nightie, the shaded lamp and the empty house at two thirty in the morning. God please save me from ever wanting to live happily ever after.

'Moira, I sometimes think that you want to live happily ever after.'

Moira stared at Magdalen, olive pinched between two immaculately manicured digits. Long thoughts.

'Bloody hell, you could be right.'

'Look I've got to go, thanks ever so for the nice drink, do take care.' Moira was silent except for the ritual 'bye bye' and, outside, Magdalen stopped in her tracks by the laurels. Something in her too still yearned to live happily ever after, but it was tempered by the knowledge that this could never be, not for anyone. Conditioning. If you became that emotionally dependant upon another, then you also became a burden, which kills love, kills life. Magdalen walked on thinking, 'Happiness anyway, it is all relative.' Not a consoling thought on a cloudy afternoon.

Indoors Moira suddenly had to run to the bathroom with a violent attack of vomiting and diarrhoea. 'Iris bloody Murdoch indeed, you'd expect better from a feminist,' but once the attack was over she returned to the sitting room, picked up *Nuns and Soldiers* and read on, riveted, until the wine was done and darkness prevented her, when she slid off into oblivion, hoping, oh I do hope Daisy will be all right in the end.

14

Clive was on a train, the royal steam engine, complete with dining car and observation platform. A crowd of courtiers and servants, relatives, friends and one or two wistful hangers on formed a party in full swing. Beautiful baked meats were laid on gold plate and fresh bread and jugs of red wine were everywhere being sampled. No white wine, Magdalen's favourite, nor salad nor any other thing. Who had done the ordering for the refreshments? He should know these things, he was too often embarrassed by not knowing what was going on in the household, getting out of it by saying it was not his side of things. Usually, he just paid for it and made no enquiry. He looked up drawn by a look and found his wife's royal gaze fixed upon him from the other end of the richly decorated carriage. Expressionless, unreadable, he did not know what face to present and found himself gazing out of the window instead.

They were crossing a stony desert in North Dakota, one of Magdalen's favourite train rides. She said the bleakness enriched her inner world, but for Clive it chilled the spirits. Blazing sunlight made long black shadows, drama everywhere. To avoid the landscape he grabbed a hunk of bread, carved a slice of bloody beef and began eating, washing it down with the strong red Burgundy wine, too good to be sloshed about in jugs perhaps; he didn't really know or care about wine.

Magdalen fought her way through the laughing crowd towards him; they should have parted respectfully for her but that was the modern world for you!

'Hello Clive. Will you break bread with me?' She offered him a fresh crust from her bread, held out her glass for him to drink from.

'Thanks all the same, I have some here,' he said, knowing this was the wrong response but not knowing anything more appropriate. He looked out of the window again to avoid the sight of Magdalen putting her offering down on the table and turning away. The train was riding a curve away from the plain, towards a mountain. The track led into a tunnel. Magdalen was hurrying, and now the crowd did part for her and she reached the observation car where she stood with her back to him. The people deliberately impeded his attempt to follow.

Magdalen waved to an invisible crowd by the tracks, head held high, and as the train went into the darkness he heard the sound of cheering.

He woke up panicking, tangled in the duvet, sweating, dropped the telephone, tried again. Got to check, got to know.

'Hello. Twelve Trees? This is Clive Hayward, can I speak to the Queen of America please?' There was a snort of disgusted disapproval.

'Mr Hayward, please, we have asked you many times not to encourage her in her fantasies. I will put you through to Mrs Hayward if you will hold for a moment.' Silly cow. Well, she must be all right if they were putting him through. They could hardly expect a corpse to come to the phone.

They took the telephone trolley to Magdalen's bedside.

'Mrs Hayward, telephone.' Magdalen thought, oh Christ, it must be Clive. Nobody else ever telephoned her. I shall be late at the college dear, keep dinner hot, pressure of work. Lying bastard.

'Hello Clive.'

'How did you know it was me?' Already forgotten the anxiety for her safety, already manifesting the tricky business of staying top.

'I'm telepathic of course. You don't need to phone, I can read your mind.' His body temperature sank several degrees until incipient frostbite of the penis brought him to his senses.

'I just thought I'd ring you anyway to see if you were all right.'

'Don't you mean "to hear" if I'm all right?'

'You could put it that way.'

'Well, am I all right?'

'I suppose you must be.'

'How kind of you to call. Was there anything else?'

'Not really. Everything's fine at home, you don't have to worry about a thing really, it's all clean and shipshape and the accounts are OK. I hired a gardener and he's done rather well, the magnolia flowered, I'll bring you a bloom if you like. How are you feeling?'

'I don't know, it's a miracle.' What?

'I had a strange dream last night.'

'The death train you mean?'

It was genuine fear, that churning in the bowels, pure noradrenalin giving him a foretaste of further hells. 'What did you say, this is a bad line?'

'Not a bad line, it led exactly where one would expect. Tell me Clive, how were your seminars on Sartre? I can't imagine you getting a good reception for him these days.'

'They were OK, none of the students had ever heard of him so I had fresh ground to plough.'

'Yes I know dear, virgin soil with every new intake of students. You know Clive, you should have no fear going through the Valley of the Shadow. Still waters run deep.' Clive began to reply but she had hung up on him.

Being a sensible person, he went downstairs to get the coffee on the go. She was alive, but still talking the most utter rubbish. If it went on another year like Woody Allen she should try Lourdes.

15

Nurse Gerhard wheeled the telephone trolley away and then returned to her own room although it was not her official break. Mrs Hayward had delusions of grandeur, but it had to be admitted that her husband was a dead loss and fit only to be hung up upon. She herself had no intention of getting married, it was a horrible trap. Five years of nursing married female mental patients had taught her that lesson.

It was not a professional attitude to call patients 'barmy' but in the case of Mrs Hayward she could not help herself. Even if she had met the woman outside the hospital she would have thought 'barmy' – anyone who had a snake tattooed up their spine emerging from the anus and its head burrowing into her hairline was barmy. Creepy, was it not?

In her room she drew the blinds, locked the door, turned on her trannie to cover sound, and went to unlock her wardrobe. Here she kept her treasures.

Shoe boxes, carefully labelled, tied with black lingerie ribbon. Scarves, knickers, bras, stockings. On the top shelf a row of black polythene bags, each containing a hat. Nurse Gerhard reached for the second from the left and from it took a large brown felt fedora hat with a brown silk scarf knotted around it in place of its original ribbon. This hat had belonged to Magdalen Hayward who still believed that it had blown from her head to oblivion on the day she arrived at the doors of Twelve Trees. A lot of things either blew away or were lost in the laundry at Twelve Trees. So Nurse Gerhard told their distressed owners.

She sat in front of her dressing table mirror and placed the hat on her stiff blonde hair. The hat transformed her completely, more than any other article in her collection. The image in the mirror was no longer herself, but that of an eccentric and dignified queen, someone like Christiana of the Netherlands perhaps, very beautiful but cold and distant, filled with a crusading spirit which burned from the eyes.

She took her hand mirror and turned her head to see first one profile and then the other. She adjusted the slant of the hat to a more becoming angle, more rakish, daring, masculine. She contemplated this self from every point. Again she faced the mirror, almost closing her eyes to blur the image, blot out imperfections in her complexion, gazing into her own eyes.

There was a humming sound, a whirring, the room became suddenly illuminated with white light. Only just in time she ripped off the hat and stuffed it back into its bag, locked it back in the wardrobe.

Everything was normal. Nurse Gerhard returned to duty, renewed in vigour, as large as life and twice as nasty.

16

It had been quiet for hours if hours there were. They hadn't
called her she hadn't called them. The nurse had not appeared,
the phone hadn't – there wasn't a phone. She would ask for one
presently and discover if it could connect to earth, and ask the
operator for the exchange she was on if the dial did not state –
and it would not state.

In human or earth terms it would not be possible to have a
telephone call over such a long distance – presumably it was a
long distance – but in their terms it would be possible. It was a
Zen conflict of the kind which she had long ago stopped trying
to reconcile – two opposing things could be true and that was all
there was to the matter. The kind of waves (or particles) which
zithered and twitched distorted messages from mouth to ear
could perhaps get messages correct, understood, over light years?

During her exile, talking on the telephone had made her feel
even more cut off in some ways, for people did not always get
the meaning of her words, even when she made great efforts to
be very clear. Even with very simple statements people were
likely to ask 'what do you mean?' and this of course taxed
Magdalen's patience, inclining her to be surly or even silent.

Would she ever return to the White House? It seemed a
remote possibility and not even desirable. She had not been
heading there when she had driven along the road by the rocks,
but had reserved all that for 'later'. Later could be very late
indeed. Just now it felt to be unthinkable, therefore she would
not think about it.

Hours had gone by and she had sat to table over the dregs and crumbs, waiting, dreaming, picking at quick and sucking the ends of her hair, considering the important matter of one kind of wallpaper as compared to another, but only in theory. Planning a dinner party perhaps; when she gave another one she might have place cards punched in computer code, simple details which made all the difference to a party! And on the other hand, no more big parties for people she did not like, she had sworn to give it up while riding across the Australian desert on a bicycle, avoiding snakes, perfectly balanced, riding and riding, pregnant, eventually giving birth and dying in a hollow in an English hill, ejecting a child into a pool of blood. Or upstairs in Golders Green, a last dinner with almonds, a birth, a marriage, another death after which she had never smiled again. Not being amused.

Could she laugh or cry? She had rather seven times seven shit in public than admit that sometimes her emotions would not work. She strained to weep and produced only belly rumblings. Struggled to laugh and only began to crack. It was the drugs they had given her for a punishment. Part of the brainwashing; they wanted her to stop believing in herself as a queen and to join the common masses, become a brother, even though she was a sister.

If Gurdjieff had been correct and laughter was the struggle of 'yes' and 'no' in the brain then if it could not come out it would have to implode; that would account for her painful liver and the backache. Was this to be yet another hypochondriac phase? Oh dear, it was enough to make one sick!

It had been an interesting hobby in its way, hypochondria; a lot of fun could be derived from visiting a library to look up symptoms only to find yet other appropriate symptoms. The best library of all for that was the British Museum medical library in Bayswater; Magdalen had spent many rapt hours in here, aided by the microfiche and the helpful librarian who always fetched exactly the right books. Working out her own treatments had been fun too, and she had always recovered, proving that doctors were not as necessary or as bloody clever as they thought. The only ailment she had found no suitable cure for was her occasional night of total sleeplessness. Drugs were a washout because of the ensuing depression and nothing else worked. She had concluded that it was caused by temporary hormonal imbalances, and that it did not matter.

These bouts of insomnia had begun when she was twelve, when she had gone to stay with her friend's aunt. The two girls had been put together in a large bed, and outside the window the moon was full and so large it seemed to fill all space. The girl's aunt who was said to have no nipples had declared that they must not gaze at the moon or they would go mad, so of course they had, for hours, disappointed when it set and they were as sane as ever.

'It didn't do anything to me at all.'

'Me neither. It's just an old wives' tale.'

'Yes. But I do feel a bit strange.'

'Funny you should say that. I was just thinking the same but didn't like to say. Sort of funny.'

'That's right. Perhaps it's a trance.'

'Yes. A trance. That's right.'

Ever since then, whether she knew it was full moon or not, Magdalen had been unable to sleep for two whole nights. When sleep did not come, she would go and draw back the heavy velvet curtains at the White House and always see a full moon. The curious thing was that this kind of not sleeping gave her energy instead of making her tired. Had she told anyone that, they would have thought her as mad as the aunt predicted.

The curtains in this room were tantalising. Perhaps this place had a moon? She got up and drew back the curtains and indeed there was a full moon; not the miraculous lights, but a huge moon. This was astonishing, but what was even more amazing was that the light of that moon shone down brilliantly onto a characteristic moon landscape.

17

She knew immediately that they were testing her. They had used a surrealist landscape to produce changed breathing, chemical shocks, so that they could record those changes and shocks. Very clever. The shining circle out there was not the moon, it could only be a moon of a moon – Gurdjieff had said that it was called Anoolios. Well, it was strange even if artificial, because she certainly had symptoms not only of full moon insomnia, but of watery tides and pressures presaging a menstrual flow. Which if it came at full moon as it often did was surely made stronger by that pull?

She and Clive had often stood gazing at the full moon after sex, eating apricot and almond tarts, and Magdalen had often wept, because of the watery tides which swamped her cells but more deeply because of the orgasms she craved and which refused to manifest even with his most detailed efforts. They were the wrong details, that was the trouble, but she dare not tell him that for he would shrink and disappear, gone with his ego.

Her distress angered him, he said it was aimed at him as a weapon, she was full of self-pity and should contain herself, as he did. How easy to do when fully satisfied. She had become ill and depressed, her soul had gone cold, solidified, and stuck in her middle regions like a lump of lead. She had wished to die.

Until one day by accident all that restrained sexual energy had exploded upwards as a molten snake, broken the gates of paradise and taken her on its wings into an hour of ecstasy that might as well have been an eternity. It had made her feel that suffering would be rewarded; a mistake in general, but in particular, sometimes and grandly.

Clive had been envious.

That had surely been the end of the beginning?

And he had no tides, denied the existence of a fire serpent with wings, scoffed at ecstasy and suspected epilepsy. And ever afterwards she was satisfied but had become one of a group; what he could do at home he wished to practise elsewhere. She bled too much, and took up Tantra crafts, meddled with black arts, retracted, read a hundred books and did not have the ecstasy again.

Would there have been any point in telling all that to the psychiatrist to whom he had eventually taken her? She thought not, although Dr Murgatroyd had at least told Clive in her presence that she was jealous and depressed because Clive neglected her. Clive had been having a deaf day, and later denied that he had been spoken to at all.

What horrible fun, the marriage game.

Magdalen felt like taking a bath. She explored and found an excellent bathroom complete with bidet which she was sure she had not requested. Her favourite scent, a sharp lemony tang, was everywhere. But there was no plug in the bath, the towels were numerous but small and square (impossible to knot into a hanging-rope) and there was no razor to shave her legs. No scissors to trim her nails. Never mind, she could stuff a flannel down the hole, the water could be topped up.

Later, feeling wonderfully relaxed, she asked for a clean scarlet nightgown and it came with white lace edges, freshly laundered and made of cotton. Her favourite nightgown, long as long and so cosy.

Outside the window now there was nothing but a greyish mist like a sea of old sour milk.

As soon as she got between the sheets she yelped and leapt out; it had been an apple-pie bed with some awful thing down there. What jokers! There came a raucous guffaw from nowhere, very like the sound of Mrs Morrison across the corridor, the poor old woman who was laughing herself to death.

The scaring object in the bed turned out to be a Rupert Bear complete with scarf and boot button eyes. Not alive of course. She rearranged the sheets and got into bed with the toy, cuddling him. She gave him a goodnight kiss as she had kissed her toys goodnight when young. After that, her sleep was long and beautiful.

18

Walking down Fifth Avenue was like a dream. It was raining, making rainbows in gasolene puddles too full to paddle. She jumped the gutters in high heels as once she had jumped in pumps after the coalman had been, for his lorry always pissed colours.

Two thousand beautiful dark people also walked down Fifth Avenue with coloured umbrellas. No noise, no placards, poor clothes. A Puerto Rican demonstration. Magdalen watched entranced as they showed themselves to the world's richest people. She joined them for a while and then returned to the sidewalk among the spectators. Feeling high she spoke without thinking to the man next to her, asking, why were they demonstrating exactly?

'We-e-ll, I doanow, bud I sure thingk id wuddabin a lod bedda aroun' heah if der Germans haddawunda wah.' After a few moments Magdalen's synapses dealt with the words and then the meaning. She did not totter, nor find a suitable reply. The man spoke again.

'Just take a look at that. Waddamezz.' Magdalen found her responses.

'I think it looks lovely in the rain, cheers up a grey day. They aren't a nuisance or anything after all.' She turned to the man smiling brilliantly, full of optimism that he was probably very nice, really. He looked at her too and his face changed. Her very dark summer tan threw him for a moment, then he saw that she was not American. He was thickset with very short bristly pale hair and pinkish skin. His neck had rolls of fat and his eyes were pale mad grey. His nostrils were wide and he was extremely clean and tough. He did not speak.

'I'm English actually, here on vacation, and I'm afraid I know almost nothing about politics.' It was a downright lie, what she meant was, 'I don't give a fuck about politics, it is a waste of brain power.'

'English huh?' He clearly doubted that she was anything as harmless as English. 'Well tell me this, lady. Doanya thingk id wuddabin a lod bedda ifan da English hadda lorst the war to Hitler? I mean, you people are overrun with niggers these days ain't ya?'

'Not really overrun. The shops have improved since we had mixed race communities but the West Indians still won't go near Sainsbury's. I don't blame them, it's a con really, rather high prices you know. I can get fresh chilli at my end of town at a quarter the price – but anyway in answer to your question no, I don't think Hitler should have won. I wouldn't be here probably, I had a half-Jewish grandma.' The man stared at Magdalen, made a disgusting disgusted noise and turned away, striding off through the people holding up his stubby head. As she stared after him he turned like a mechanical doll and came back, thrusting himself up close.

'Ledd me tell you lady my father was German and he should know, you wuz only a kid during the war, right? Iddadavbin a lodd bedda, believe me.' Then he strode away again, this time in the opposite direction.

Magdalen swallowed the experience, thinking, so much for a subtle understanding of Nietzsche. Did that pig appreciate Wagner? She herself listened to it in much the same way as she listened to Rasta music which she loved, at the same time finding the underlying philosophy repellant. Not without negative allure, a similar approach to pre-Raphaelite painting was necessary for her also. She didn't have to languish to death to find Millais' *Ophelia* wonderful. What went on in men like him? Did he really want to gas everyone who wasn't a so called Aryan? It was scary.

The demonstration had gone and the windows of the shops were so artistically dressed that there were few goods to look at. Bored and with tired feet she found a little coffee bar to rest herself in for a while. She sat down with two large black transport workers. She smiled and so did they, watching with interest as she rolled herself a cigarette. Would men *never* get used to women rolling cigs and drinking pints? Hell, Dietrich had done it years ago in that movie with James Stewart, and Blavatsky did it all the time before the turn of the century. Exceptions of course, and these men probably had never heard of Blavatsky.

'Have you ever heard of Madame Blavatsky?' she asked upon an impulse.

'I think so, isn't that the little deli at the corner of West 85th?'

'Nah, that's Kerensky's. What kinda shop is it, like a dress and hats place?'

'No, it's a person in history. Nobody knows of her these days.'

'What she do?'

'She invented a crazy religion.'

'Lotta those about today. Dem Rastas sure crazy.'

'Dey used say dat 'bout Pentecostal, now it's respectable OK.'

'Takes time. Hey lady you on vacation from England?'

'That's right. And I like it here.'

'The city's a bad place for a woman alone. Now don't you go on out at night alone.'

'Oh nothing scares me.'

'They say that till they get mugged. I ain't kidding.'

'Well thanks for the warning, I'll take care.'

'You gotta terrible war on over dere dat so?'

'I hadn't noticed. Not in England.'

'You know, Ireland and Wales. Da Warraderroses.'

'Oh that! That's North and South Ireland, not actually England.'

'But da British Isles is all one place, dat I do know.'

'Well yes, but England isn't in the war. Well not exactly.'

'I'm sure glad to know that. Last time you people

haddawarweall came over there to help. Bad news.'

'Bad news indeed.' Magdalen saw that the Italian barman was trying to catch her eye; was she being pestered? She looked away. Hardly pestered, but she would be if she let him intervene in the chat. Italians never missed an opportunity to try for a woman. Magdalen didn't like them; they were too much talk and not enough action.

Eventually she felt strong enough to walk some more, and wandered on foot all the way back to West 88th.

The flat was stuffy and humid, the fan was broken and opening windows didn't help at all. Nowhere to go tonight, dates tomorrow. Rest, facepack, bathe, read. She opened up the double bed between its two awful bronze statuettes, got together a relaxing kit which was all her smoking equipment, a dish of washed apples and a pile of books. A long shower later she lay back as darkness fell. The room was very strange, with the least sympathetic décor of any she had ever encountered. Even the handles on the fake French antique drawers had cutting edges, and the dust on the maple leaves in the fireplace obscured all their colours. But it was free, she had been lent it by a friend of a friend, so she did not feel like complaining.

She began reading Herman Hesse, found the theatre not very magical. Someone knocked at the door making her jump and drop the book. The three locks, one with an iron bar, were all secure. She had been warned never to leave her door open. Who?

'It's me, Leyland from upstairs.' Oh. She had been introduced to him on arrival, and told she was welcome to socialise or take her problems to him, but had been too shy. He was very attractive but being married she had found herself shy.

He came in and sat by the dusty leaves, smiling. His smile showed brilliant because he was black.

'I just dropped by to see if there was anything I could do for you.' Wow! 'I've got a bottle of whisky upstairs if you feel like a drink.' Hell!

'Not really thanks, I'm tired. I'm just relaxing this evening but it is nice of you to ask.' What a fool she felt, lying in a double bed in her bathrobe, with a beautiful young man sitting there offering whisky, and refusing. How life had changed, how alienating an object was a wedding ring.

'Yeah, the city can be tiring until you get used to it, but a drink revives.' She didn't respond but asked some polite questions about his life. He was an actor, been through acting school on a grant after doing Vietnam. Yes it was true, they sent the blacks to the dangerous parts first. He'd been lucky to return alive.

'They're very nosy in this place, when I bring a friend of mine here he dresses in full African robes, all the doors open all the way up the stairs. And next to you is Moxie. She's crazy, stays in all the time just drinking. And there's a man with a Dobermann, that dog will kill anyone, very dangerous. Someday he'll fall down dead and that dog will get loose and kill. You've got interesting neighbours, keep your door shut.'

'I let you in, is that OK?'

'I'm harmless. Now, if you were a young man as beautiful as you are now, I might just be considered a nuisance, depending on the reaction.' She laughed before she realised what she was laughing at; laughing at your own repressed disappointment causes stomach ache, Magdalen realised. Good and beautiful men were very scarce, it seemed a pity that so many of them were gay. She offered him an apple.

'Now that's a temptation I can't resist,' he said, coming over to the bed. He was just taking an apple from the bowl she held out when everything went dark.

'Oh Lord, a fuse again. These old buildings, there are so many fuses. People put too much equipment on all at the same time. I'll go and mend it, I usually do.' He set off for the cellar, feeling his way in the dark, amongst the sounds of doors opening, shouts of wrath and the howls of a dog. Magdalen slammed her door against the Dobermann, terrrified. A scurry of claws and a blood-curdling howl made her cringe. She found her lighter and lit up the candles. It improved the décor.

What a ninny she was, really. Letting a guy go mend a fuse, not even thinking to do it herself. And being afraid of a dog. She wasn't really scared of dogs; she could telepath things to them such as good boy and hello dog. But then, it surely wasn't just her who would be scared in a strange apartment building in New York if the lights went out and a reputedly murderous Dobermann came howling? Lots of people, men as well, would be scared in such a situation. And she didn't know where the fuses were and she didn't know anything about American electrics either; here, they had two silly bits of metal instead of a proper wall-plug. But it was no good pretending to herself about this situation, because the crux was that, at home, she had always let Clive mend fuses and deal with domestic disasters. So it was stupid to expect anything else from herself until she learned to do the damn things herself. Preferably without the dog, telepathy notwithstanding.

She felt blood come wet and realised, goodness, this is the first time for many years I haven't been really ill before a period. No warnings except a slight fear – this was good. When she was away by herself she didn't get physically ill with anything it seemed. Sometimes she had suspected Clive of sucking all her energy from her in the night and making her weak and ill but of course most people would have thought that sheer paranoia. She took a candle into the bathroom and washed herself by its soft light. Men *did* take your energy, men *did* make you ill sometimes, just by being close all the time.

'I love you my pretty maid.'

'Well prithee sir, why do I not feel better for it?'

A very good question. Bronchitis, backache, rashes, symptoms unknown to science loosely classed as 'women's ailments', the kind of thing which made doctors dread their approach for did they not make them feel impotent, irritated? Seven years at medical school in order to repeatedly prescribe Diazepam. But not now, hardly at all. Progress was being made, perhaps. Jesus, *anybody* could get tired and spooked in New York City!

There was a rattling at the door.

'It's me again, I've fixed the fuse.' She let him in, thinking, I bet he makes somebody's earth move. He held out a large blown fuse like a used firework. They both laughed.

66

'I'd better leave you to your reading and rest then. Don't forget, if you're lonely or want any help, I'm upstairs, right at the top.' She thanked him and laboriously locked up, then lay on the bed in the steaming hot night repressing a violent desire to masturbate. It was all very well being guiltless and the owner of your own body, but it usually gave you a headache and a sense of futility.

She was wakened from sleep by a thundering on the door. Someone else, complaining that there was a flood of water coming through the ceiling. She got up and looked everywhere but found no leaks.

'It's got to be your apartment, it's wetting the sofa. Let me in, I want to look.'

'Listen, there are no leaks, and you may have a flood, but even if it's Armageddon I'm not letting you in here in the middle of the night.' Silence, then retreat. In New York you had to learn to dish it out. From behind a triple-locked door. If she'd had a man with her, would she have let him deal with situations such as this? She half suspected that she would. And then thought, well, maybe not, not any more. There was no man, it remained to be tested.

Suddenly profoundly depressed she slunk back to bed and produced an unsatisfactory orgasm. Where was the real Magdalen? Gone forever? Hell and hell, this was an awful state to be in.

On the other hand, she needed sleep, and in the morning everything would seem different. With luck.

19

Magdalen awoke to find herself looking at her own distorted reflection in a dome of molasses before the inevitable childish fingerprint spoiled the image. The treacle moved away, an eye, the eye of the alien insect huge and watchful. She was being examined as a specimen.

'You startled me,' she said quietly. The thing lifted up its huge sticky pads and made gestures which might have meant anything, but it said, 'Oh, sorry.'

She slowly sat up in bed and the Rupert Bear fell on its head on the floor. The creature picked up the bear and tenderly tucked it in beside her again. Magdalen could have wept at the human sentimentality.

'I was watching over you, I do hope you don't feel intruded upon.'

She felt intruded upon. 'No of course not.'

'I was observing your rapid eye movements.'

'Every ninety minutes according to research done on earth.'

'We have no time. Here, you dream constantly.'

Well, that was different anyway. Dream constantly.

'You realise of course that research you do upon me here will not be valid, in the sense that time is all important where I used to reside?'

'We can fill in from your storage system which seems to be very efficient except that your own access to it doesn't work correctly.'

'You mean I forget things?'

'Precisely. We find this strange. If we forget anything we have to be treated as sick. We cannot see the use of a memory bank if its owner cannot use the stored material.' Neither could Magdalen, but the idea of being able to remember everything all at once was incomprehensible. She could remember everything, but not a telephone number when she needed it, or the capital of Zanzibar, if there was still such a place.

Magdalen cuddled Rupert and regarded the alien. She wanted to go outside of this room and there must be a way to get its consent to that. Had they said she could go soon, that they were constructing her a suit?

'Do you think I could explore outside a bit today please? I'm getting bored you know, it isn't good for me.'

'Your suit is not ready yet, but to keep you company we've decided to bring another of your kind.'

Good grief, who? It was like those sixties dinner parties where whites who knew two blacks would invite them both to dinner and be puzzled that they didn't like one another. A Nigerian professor of linguistic philosophy and a Jamaican sugar-cane worker. Some conversation.

She had said nothing, had gone into reverie.

'Are you not delighted at the prospect of company?'

'Eh? Oh! Sure. Depends who of course.'

'We thought we could bring your mate. We need to see humans breeding.' Her laughter echoed round three galaxies.

'Is that funny?'

'Hilarious! He couldn't possibly do it if he was watched. Mostly he likes the light out when there's only the two of us. You don't realise what a fragile and sensitive thing a penis can be.'

'That is true.'

'You see, if two human beings are locked up together for a longish time, even if they begin by loving one another, then eventually that love turns to hate.'

'That is very unfortunate. Well, a visitor for you seems a good idea, but perhaps for a short piece of your "time"?'

'Yes. I'm sure that might be a good idea.'

20

'In all the meta-Pragues of my active mind, the streets are grey and damp with grease from people long walked away. Green blinds hide the neurosis of the store fronts and sometimes dust-devils haunt the gutters, foretelling rain which never comes until there is a feast day. Hot dog stands give off an odour of warm rotting onions that curdles the stomach and taints the hair, so that if one were ever kissed, the kiss would be spoiled by something not quite identifiable but infinitely repellant. "She reminds me of evil" some prospective seducer would vaguely think, and be put off evil which he had planned. Thus hot dogs have their roll in secular religious activity.'

She tore the sheet of paper into two and let them float away on either side of her. Mrs Thornton came over to her, smiling and reproachful, her brows creased and her mouth smiling, a contradiction which was meant to convey sympathetic interest.

'Now why do you tear your poem Magdalen my dear?' Every syllable was controlled, long practice in not exciting aggression in lunatics, first requisite of the occupational therapist.

'Because it's a load of shit is why. And it's prose, I hate poetry most of the time.'

'Oh well, if it's as bad as that dear perhaps you were right to tear it up. But I would like to read it. May I?' She was already piecing the destroyed prose together, a simple puzzle to solve.

As she read, Magdalen watched her eyes moving from side to

side in the scrubbed face with fine red veins. Dry wayward greying hair, washed so often it had gone down the plughole in little bits. The skin on her knuckles was shiny with soap and scrubbing, the nails whitened with a pencil, no rings except the very worn gold band, which might as well have been a set of chains. Magdalen's English mistress had had nails like Mrs Thornton's. She had been the daughter of a 'Sir' and had been an epitome of middle-class decency and grace and perfect cleanliness, except that her breath smelled. The girls had known that under her very expensive clothes there lurked whalebone corsets, for she had made the mistake of asking two girls to fetch them from a corsetiers one tea time. Pale pink, busks, whalebone, steel springs, lacings, hooks. Garments of terror and torture but her outline when in them was without fault. But her breath gave her away.

They knew that when she took off those corsets her abdomen would expand, rumbling and gaseous, a horrendous Zeppelin of middle-class foods suppurating: steak and kidney pie, overdone Brussels, mashed potatoes, cream sauce, sponge pudding, custard, white bread, the perfect culture medium for cancer of the bowel. She had never smoked or touched alcohol, never been near a man, she was beautifully dressed but with tea and three sugars, chocolates and Madeira cake, her temple was defiled. However, she had known her English grammar and encouraged the use of the imagination. She had opened doors into Wordsworth and Magdalen had entered into a world of (temporary) pantheism.

'Mrs Thornton, what would you say if I told you we were on another planet, captured by aliens?' Mrs Thornton put down the paper and leaned forward, conspiratorially.

'Ssh. The others might hear and be upset. They think they are in the Creative Writing class at Twelve Trees. I thought I was the only one to know what was really going on.'

Magdalen screeched laughing but managed to quell it as heads turned. Mrs Thornton was very red with giggling.

'You are humouring me,' hissed Magdalen and Mrs Thornton shook her head, no, not at all.

'They make wonderful simulacra of places sometimes, just to make you feel at home,' Magdalen heard her teacher say. 'As a matter of fact dear, I am writing a science fiction novel about my sojourns with them, the problem being to make it credible within its own parameters. I had thought of doing it from the point of view of a mental hospital patient, so that people could have a choice of realities, if you follow me.'

'I do, I do. I don't think it would work as a travel book, not if it is the same planet as I go to, and it would seem to be if you are here.'

'Exactly. The creatures there are like tiny insects.'

'You mean the creatures here.'

'No I do not, you know perfectly well where we are, a joke is a joke.'

'But you just gave yourself away Mrs Thornton. Go on, describe the insect creatures.' Mrs Thornton hesitated, then looked dreamily over Magdalen's head.

'They have three eyes and a snout and lovely soft paddy paws but they are very adept with them, and extremely intelligent. They enjoy semantic games and transmit matter from one form to another directly. The can create things out of my imagination. I said I would like to go to Istanbul for my holiday this year and instantly there I was, wandering around the great market in the heat of summer. Also, their lobster mayonnaise is out of this world.' Magdalen was silenced, but caught herself trying to rationalise this coincidence much as Dr Murgatroyd did. Telepathy for example. But was that a rational explanation? Mrs Thornton picked up Magdalen's writing again.

'It is a shame you tore your writing. I like it.'

'I want to talk about . . .'

'I am paid to help you in this class dear. Be a good girl and concentrate. I'll get the sack if anyone realises what we were just talking about. Or be turned into a patient.' They giggled like schoolgirls, causing heads to turn again.

The patients looked upon Mrs Thornton as a sympathetic ear and ally against some of the nursing staff, and her class was more popular than basket making because she could be trusted with personal information. All the work was locked away in a filing cabinet each week and Mrs Thornton put the keys in her handbag and took them home; this was very reassuring for nobody wanted nurses and doctors reading their private work.

'It's really very good, I find it a little bit inaccessible to criticism.'

Magdalen felt a warm wave of satisfaction. 'I don't actually see how you can understand it because it is very personal and doesn't say much.'

'People said that about Kafka's work, and others. Let's go through it and see if you are communicating.'

'All right.'

'The beginning is full of mystery and shows that you travel to many places in your mind. Not much jollity or love in this one. Kafka was good at this sort of thing but most people do not appreciate his humour. Is this meant to be funny?'

'Oh yes. Sort of hilarity at being detached from awful surroundings and in them at the same time. I fall about on the floor laughing when I read Kafka.'

'That's what Kafka did when writing, isn't that nice? I expect he would have been pleased, he was not as estranged as people think, so many get depressed reading him.'

'He was probably surrounded by strange people with a rigid sense of humour.'

'All too likely. I'm a bit bothered about greasy streets and dust-devils. . . .' Here Magdalen thought for a moment that Mrs Thornton was rambling but recovered on realising that the images were from her bit of writing. 'You don't get damp grease and dust-devils together, but separately the images are splendid.'

'Crikey, I never thought of that. Of course not, it would stick in lumps wouldn't it? I guess I'm thinking of various depressing evenings, some in a dry March and some in a nasty November. Does it make it all right that it isn't real life therefore it doesn't have to be consistent – no of course it doesn't, no, that's dodging, isn't it?'

'It sounds a bit like it. You can invent worlds in fiction but they have to be consistent within themselves. To have dust-devils and grease you'd have to invent new worlds, you know, science fiction, and it would all have to fit and you'd have to show the reasons.'

'Could do. But this isn't exactly like that. I'll change it. I think I'll stick with the grease.'

'Good. You have to be prepared to change things to get it right. The hot dog stand in a deserted city epitomises loneliness for me, I do think that is well chosen. The smell of old fried onions – it is supposed to cheer you up but it makes you feel worse, is that what you mean?'

'Precisely.'

'Probably behind the shutters people are eating to cheer themselves up, and if you are outside in the drizzle that makes you feel worse too.' Magdalen could see that Mrs Thornton and she had far more in common than she had thought.

'And yet in that greyness you dare to think about being kissed by a seducer, but because you know that in real life encounters in the street are rarely pleasant, you go down further.' Magdalen nodded, in unison with the frizzled head. Mrs Thornton gazed into the distance, and continued with her interpretation, and it sounded as if she spoke from the meta-Prague itself.

'Yes. Any woman alone in a deserted street will attract a prospective seducer, some wretched male in a dirty mac with old-fashioned shoes and bad breath. The kind of piteous creature who masturbates alone in a room which has no real comfort. He will think of women as evil because they make him masturbate, and he thinks of that as evil. Some of them finish up murdering innocent women, expiating their own imaginary sins.' Magdalen did not interrupt, Mrs Thornton seemed to be in a trance.

'Tell me, did you make this pun "rolls" intentionally?'

'I didn't think of it in advance, it just came out. Sometimes I think in puns for hours at a time, everything has double and treble meanings and rhymes sometimes.'

'Yes I know. It's supposed to be a symptom of something, but Joyce must have suffered from it quite badly in that case.' They both laughed.

'Well, do you find my interpretation anywhere near your intention?'

'Very near.'

'Well then it's all right. Just carry on with it, see where it leads.'

'I will, and thanks very much.' When Mrs Thornton had gone Magdalen put the two pieces of paper back in the waste-paper basket. She didn't want to write much really, she came here to check that there were still ordinary people who understood her at all. The trouble was that when she found someone who did understand, they turned out not to be very ordinary after all.

21

Clive Hayward was conducting a philosophy tutorial with one of his dimmer male students. The time allotted for a serious discussion of the broader points of the Descartes primer was a further twenty minutes. So far they had managed to discuss the dreadfully boring décor of the college corridors, how depressing it was walking down them, and the possibility of arranging a disco in the student common room for the next night with a bar which would serve until one in the morning. The student, Stuart Baines, had said that nothing was impossible if you believed in it and Clive had called that nothing but magic practice. There was a difference between concept and reality. Not, replied Stuart, if you strengthened your concept and thus altered reality. Clive felt vaguely sympathetic with this which he had called 'enthusiasm' but knew that the police had to be approached three weeks in advance for a liquor licence and that they would not understand or care about concept.

And discos were nothing to Clive.

'You know Stuart, your thesis is not really progressing as it should be. Not only is the word count ludicrously low but the quality of your expression lets you down all the way through. You have to aim at absolute clarity, you can't write this kind of thing as if it were a mystical utterance.'

'Well, the way I see it, the only way to convey philosophy is through mystical utterance.'

'You aren't conveying philosophy. You are trying to prove that you thoroughly understand the way in which others have conveyed it before you, and that you understand the material they have conveyed.' Stuart actually groaned aloud.

'Do you want your degree or not?'

'I suppose so, but when you think about it, a degree in philosophy isn't going to do me much good in life anyway, is it?'

Clive always dreaded this question.

'As far as getting a job goes no, but you were warned of that earlier. Philosophy is a training for the mind, and therefore one might say that it will help you in whatever discipline you follow.'

'Not this old crap.'

'What do you want to do with your life?'

'I plan to travel around the world for a few years after I get out of here and experience some real life. This isn't real life after all, is it?'

'It is one form of real life. It is as real as any other life you might lead but possibly not as exciting. Are you beginning to tell me that you intend to drop out?'

'We don't use that expression any more. I just intend to travel and see the world while it is still there to be seen.' Clive did not know how to reply. He would rather like to do that himself, but not at the expense of losing his post here at the college.

'And I might write books.'

'Well you will jolly well have to find ways of making your meanings more clear than you do now, you are quite incomprehensible at times, and display a disgraceful illiteracy. You are not of course the only one, most students can hardly spell and haven't a clue what syntax is.'

'What is syntax? Should I care? For a new age we need a new grammar.'

'That's bullshit. If I were you I'd be inclined to drop out – er – travel right now instead of waiting for a failed degree.'

'I can't, my folks will stop my money if I do that.'

'So you have a practical streak. Good. Now, I want three thousand words on chapter two, coherent, reasoned, thought out, researched, backed up by argument, for next Thursday. Is that clear?'

'Very.' He left. Then returned.

'When did you say you wanted all that stuff for?'

'Next Thursday. Wait a minute. Do you take drugs? I shall not reveal any secrets, it just occurred to me that your way of thinking is rather like the acid droppers way back in the sixties.'

'Yes, actually, but not acid. I only approve of natural herbs. Acid is man-made.'

'Well the way I understood it, it occurs in nature in a particularly nasty fungus growing on rye.'

'Yes. But we take magic mushrooms, and weed of course.'

'Do you realise you are damaging your brain by taking things like that? It has been shown that actual chromosomal changes take place. –' He stopped at the look on the boy's face.

'Do you realise that you are preventing your brain from reaching its full potential by refusing to open it up with a natural herb which grows for that purpose? Have you ever considered changed human consciousness as the next logical evolutionary step? Obviously the most intelligent people will wish to experiment with herbs and long for higher states of being, it even stands up to ordinary logic. Here, have some.' He put down his books and got a plastic bag from an inner pocket. From it he tipped onto Clive's blotter a handful of tiny dried mushrooms, and then beside that he placed a little foil-wrapped package. 'Black Ash that. Excellent stuff.'

'But this is illegal. Put it away and go away. And anyway I haven't the least idea what to do with any of it.'

'Ah. Well, I'll give you the instructions. I'm trusting you of course.' Clive writhed. He should ring the dean of course. But Magdalen had taken mushrooms once or twice, maybe more often for all he knew, with some crazy friends she'd met years ago in Wales. It was possibly the reason she had gone mad. Had a nervous breakdown. But he could hardly tell this child that.

In the silence of his unmade decision Clive knew that his wife was not nor had ever been mad, she had simply been in a different state of consciousness to himself. Perhaps if he took this stuff he would be able to meet her on her own ground? Either that or they would go further apart, how could he tell?

'You know, it isn't just for kicks. From a mushroom trip you get what you deserve and what you set up for. Like, a religious maniac has a religious experience and a music fanatic has amazing musical experiences and so on.' Clive had heard it all before. He didn't need any of that, he rejected it as being beneath him. It was therefore as if someone other than himself replied,

'Well, that's very generous of you – but you must on no account speak of this to anyone or I shall lose my job. What do you do – eat it all?'

'You could but the best way is to boil the mushrooms in two cupfuls of water with a teabag for a few minutes then strain. You get a chemical reaction with the tannin which makes it stronger. They are best taken on the night of the full moon. The dope you crumble into a home rolled cig or smoke in a pipe or you can eat a bit with some chocolate. Go steady until you know what you are looking for. Most tyros say that "nothing happens" – it's like your first drinks, you never notice anything.' Clive recalled his first drinks – stolen sherry on New Year's Eve at a friend's house – the two of them had been awake and giggling all night, convinced that they were not drunk at all. Later had come the usual vomiting, reeling and hilarity with wit. Drunkenness was learned. But you still couldn't do it without alcohol.

'Are you sure it isn't dangerous?'

'A few people seem to get bad effects but they're usually the ones who get bad effects from everything. You know, the disaster area type.' Clive laughed, knowing what was meant, and also increasingly convinced that Magdalen was not one of them. His mind always went round and round when thinking of her 'problems' – a vicious circle of effects and causes which always got him very confused.

'But you know, it is certainly true that you do not apply yourself to work.'

'I was worse before I tripped. I had no direction whatsoever.'

'And what is your direction now?'

'It only makes sense to me. You must find your own direction.' Clive felt like a student with a teacher.

He peered at the mushrooms on his blotter and heard the door close as the youth left. These plants were not illegal at least, it was the other stuff which could lose him his job, his house, his car. Or if not quite that, he could certainly be blacklisted in all sorts of subtle ways – the thing was of course not to get caught. His door burst open and in came Miriam Goldsmith with her violet hair, pearly face, dressed in gold shorts over sky-blue tights and gold football boots. His temperature went up, there was something about this basically repellant image which excited Clive, and his guilt showed not in quick reflexes but in an attitude of frozen horror.

'Ooh Clive – I didn't know you were a mushroomy sort!'

Her blouse was scattered with sequins, the sort of thing which had decorated Clive's mother's evening dresses. She had kissed him goodnight before going out to a dinner dance, smelling wonderful, and he had reached up to be kissed and to touch the sequins. She had gently removed his fingers from her breasts.

'I'm not. These were an unsolicited gift and I do not quite know what to do with them.'

'Brew up and take them on the night of a full moon of course. They reveal things.'

'So does reading a book.' Miriam ignored Clive's silly remark and went on to state that mushrooms were a natural thing, and that cannabis was nothing more than a herb.

'So are aconite and hemlock. I suppose you drink those regularly too.'

'Dark of the moon for those,' she countered, slamming her thesis down on the desk contemptuously, scattering mushrooms.

'Ooops.' Together they picked them up and she emptied a matchbox and stuffed them all in together.

'How's it going?' Clive nodded at the thesis.

'Finished, except of course you will want me to re-do lots of it. But from my point of view at the moment 'tis done.' Ages ahead, this girl worked at least.

'Well I'll look at it as soon as possible.'

'Good. Are you going to the common room disco?'

'It won't be happening, trouble with the licence.'

'No trouble. I got Daddy to fix it.'

Daddy? Of course, town councillor, politician, magistrate, County God-knew what, builder, import-export, filthy rich and powerful daddy. He gave huge sums of money to the university and the polytechnic for equipment and had founded a travelling scholarship in the geography department. Miriam would get a first and they always got a liquor licence if she wanted one. He hadn't reckoned with Miriam.

'Well yes in that case. Haven't been dancing for ages.'

'Well don't mushroom first, it's a waste. It is a full moon but I think first trips should be taken in the quiet company of an experienced tripper or more, and not out in noise and so on. Too confusing, can ruin the imagery. Some people regard these things as sacred, it is after all thousands of years old, mushroom taking.' Well, he knew that of course, but he hadn't known it was full moon the night of the disco. He was obviously out of touch with nature, whatever that really was.

'Well, I think the only person I'd really want to take them with would be my wife, and unfortunately that isn't possible, she's away.'

'Really? I saw her in town yesterday, I got these tights at the same counter in John Lewis.' Clive went cold.

'What colour was she buying?' he weirdly asked.

'Saffron. Why?'

'I don't know.'

She stared at him.

'You look ill. Didn't you think she was in town?'

'No.'

'Has she left you or something?'

'She's been in hospital a long time and she left the hospital without being declared cured and nobody knows where she is. You see. Please don't say anything, it sounds so strange, people don't understand.'

'I know. But she was fine yesterday. We spoke but not much.'

'What was she wearing?'

'Jeans and shirt. Come to think of it the tights were odd for her because I've never seen her in a skirt.' Clive rarely saw

81

Magdalen in a skirt either, to his regret. He felt his eyes full of tears. They were tears of anger. How dare she make a fool of him like this?

'Can we pack in this tutorial now please? I don't feel up to it at all.'

Miriam came round the desk and placed a motherly arm around Clive's shoulders and hugged him for a moment before leaving silently.

With a noble effort, Clive stopped his tears, swallowed his anger. It did not occur to him for a moment that he might have been glad to know that Magdalen was alive and well enough to purchase tights in a department store. Instead, he rang two colleagues and suggested lunch out at a country pub renowned for its home-made pies. They also sold excellent real ale.

There was no point in getting upset about things which could not be attended to immediately. Magdalen would return to him eventually, and *then* they would see.

22

'You will be pleased to hear that we have completed your protective suit. You may explore around today, if you wish.'

Magdalen leapt up from the table where she had been slumped over coffee dregs, very bored.

'Oh goody, where is it?'

'In your clothes cupboard.' She hurried over and found the suit. It was a vivid blue with a warm texture and furry boots and a sort of hood with goggles. It fitted perfectly and was very comfortable. Not at all claustrophobic as she had imagined.

'Am I wearing it properly, is it safe to go outside now?'

'Yes. The door is open into the airlock, and further on you will find the outer door. You are quite safe, but proceed with caution because of new experiences.'

New experiences – caution? Eagerly she went out and found a corridor with a polished wooden floor, a chair, and a table bearing an ashtray and a pile of *Country Life* magazines. Acclimatisation of course. At the far end of the corridor were double doors with portholes, and when she peered through one she saw a blank pale green wall. Oh.

But outside the doors was a corridor going two ways; she turned right, another set of doors, another.

And then she was truly in another world.

The light was horribly bright. She peeped through her lashes at the brilliant new surroundings. It was very hard to get bearings in so much light. The floor beneath was very hard and wet looking, a sort of cream stone or tile.

'Hoy-oy!' Her voice echoed dull. From what did it echo? The goggles were curved and shaded, making nonsense of shapes, unless the goggles were OK and the shapes were nonsensical. Before her stretched blueness, with beautiful patterns moving through very slowly. There was a strange smell that was familiar but she could not put a name to it – not very pleasant. Their air must be this stuff – and yet the helmet was supposed to protect her from that. But she felt fine, no need to worry.

If this was their planet it seemed curiously blank and devoid of life. She stood assessing the place, disappointed. Had she hoped for a teeming city street full of strange life forms, a jungle of exotic animals and plants? Not consciously, she had kept an open mind.

Then Magdalen heard soft sounds, a lapping like kittens drinking milk. Behind the sound was her own breathing and heartbeat. And a faint humming. Impossible to detect from what direction any outer sound had its source. Which way to go? In front of her the huge blue floor, very attractive, as if the sky had been laid down like a fitted carpet. She saw steps at the far end of what now looked like a huge patio. She felt herself beginning to smile as she gathered confidence, a rising happiness at the thought of freedom. She was not confined to the one room any more, it was marvellous. In her own America there was nothing like this. Nowhere on earth had she ever encountered such a landscape. She skipped a couple of steps, exuberant. Explorers must adapt themselves constantly, she told herself proudly, waving her arms around. She reached the edge of the blue and put a foot out to test. Nothing. There was some kind of step down – the goggles were not very good for vision.

She could not judge distances properly – but maybe their distance was different as well as their time – maybe time and space interacted to alter everything! Brilliant! Feeling like a new Einstein she stepped forward joyfully, heading for the distant steps and immediately overbalanced, tumbling with a yell. It was quite incomprehensible, it was like a free fall, it must have less gravity; she was head over heels, sinking slowly, finding everything suddenly cold. She felt wet she was so cold.

Magdalen relaxed to see what would happen and realised that the atmosphere was entirely different here, her mouth felt full of solid matter, her nostrils stung, her eyes stung, there began a ringing in her ears. The suit must not work properly. Help! The more she shouted the more she choked on the atmosphere. Where were they, did they know she was in trouble?

She floundered trying to find a way out but now there were blobs and stars in front of her eyes, there was nothing to grasp and it began to get dark. She was rapidly drawn backwards, horizontally, happily relaxing after all. Perhaps this was the airlock proper, and now indeed she would enter a new world.

The next she knew she was face down vomiting with somebody kneeling on her, then she was turned over roughly and a horrible face descended upon her scream and kissed her as if to devour. She tried to fight but had no strength in her limbs. There was a lot of noise, bellowing, echoing.

The person let go of her and began pounding her ribs, and someone was rubbing her hands and feet.

'She's all right now. Get her onto the stretcher.' Magdalen began to shiver and weep.

'How the devil did she get in here anyway, this pool door is supposed to be locked except when the instructor and two guards are present.' Nasty officious voice.

'I can't imagine. Someone came to fix the filter this morning, maybe it didn't get checked after the workmen left.'

'Somebody will be in trouble for this.'

'If I hadn't remembered I'd left my briefcase in here yesterday during staff swim period she'd have drowned.'

'Very lucky that. Do you hear, you – you're a very lucky girl.' Magdalen got it all, wearily saw what had happened, how they would interpret everything.

She pretended to be unconscious.

She felt very weary, not so much physically but because of an air of *déjà vu* about things, covering the same experience over and over – and not getting much further. A sense of disappointment hid itself behind her closed eyes, tinged with failure.

'Open your eyes Mrs Hayward, I can see you are pretending.

I've got some nice hot Ovaltine here for you, and a little prick.' Magdalen grinned, thinking, stick the little prick up your cunt, but submissively rolled over and had it jammed in her arse. Not an expert jabber. She was propped up and offered the Ovaltine.

'Doctor is coming to see you.'

'I don't feel like talking.'

'Never mind that. Dr Murgatroyd is very nice.'

Nurses loved doctors. Magdalen could not understand this, unless it was the allure of a huge salary to wed.

'That will be all Nurse thank you.' Dr Murgatroyd had arrived all gleaming and neat with a thick folder of notes, intending to add more pages. The nurse left with a brilliant smile at the doctor and a look of contempt for Magdalen all signalled in three seconds flat.

'And how are we feeling after our little dip?'

'You fell in too?'

'Very witty, but do you not recall asking me to address you at all times with the royal "we"?'

'Nothing is impossible. You may drop it, it sounds terribly patronising the way you say it.'

'I perceive that you are not too bad.'

'Could be worse, how are you?'

'Very well thank you – a bit tired, I'm very busy you know.'

'Yes, I can imagine. When did you last have sexual relations with your wife?'

'Well, we haven't – Mrs Hayward, I'll ask the questions!'

'That would make the relationship very one sided if you don't mind my saying so.'

'Well it is my job to find out why you attempted suicide and it isn't your job to find out anything about me, is it?'

'Maybe not but I don't like talking about personal matters to strangers. Would you? And I did not attempt suicide, I went exploring in a space-suit, I was on a distant planet and had got tired of being indoors.'

Dr Murgatroyd hid behind scribbling motions for a while then took a deep breath.

'A distant planet? How do you explain being here this afternoon then?'

'I can't. Can you?' He looked over his glasses at her but it didn't work; she sipped her Ovaltine and sweetly asked him for a cigarette which he supplied and lighted.

'I had thought you were making progress and that it would be perfectly all right for you to have the freedom of the place to provide stimulus. I was wrong.'

'If the suit had been efficient I could have explored.'

'Don't be silly Magdalen, that was your après-ski suit and goggles as you well know.'

'I've never skied in my life and don't intend to.'

'Well where did it come from then?'

'Out of the cupboard in the room.'

'That cupboard over there?'

'No, on the other planet.' He sighed, made notes.

Magdalen thought, it really must have been a vivid dream, I can see that what I say isn't good sense. But what was an après-ski suit doing amongst her clothes then?

'I'm worried that you might make a successful suicide attempt in error. You want to live don't you?'

'Yes of course. I've hardly ever felt really suicidal and even then I was too cowardly to act.' More notes.

'Let's see – no children. Do you think much about your husband?'

'I think of my husband with his girlfriends. I know he has them, he's always been unfaithful you know.'

'That can't be pleasant for you. Do you love him?'

'I don't get the chance. I did. I don't know.' It was the first time in her life that she had expressed doubt on that subject. It was frightening, but clean.

'Are you trying to punish him into being faithful?'

'Not as far as I know. It wouldn't be any good even if I knew how to do that. He doesn't love me.'

'Are you sure?'

'Well if he does, I don't feel any better for it.'

'I see.'

'Do you? Do you love your wife?'

'Of course.'

'That means you don't. "Of course" is a defensive reply.'

'When you are better perhaps you might consider seven years training to become a psychiatrist?'

'What, so's I can sit by some poor sod's bed making sarcastic comments?'

'Oh dear. Look, let's begin again.'

'OK. What's in those notes?'

'Reminders for myself later.'

'A dossier. It will go into a computer and be used as evidence against me if I ever speed in a car or get caught crossing a border with dope. Dr Murgatroyd wrote 'paranoia still evident' and then he added 'if she isn't taking the piss out of me'.

'Well Magdalen, a fresh start. Could you say if you have some deep unhappiness in you that you could begin to express in words? She thought and felt and could have wept for it was true, she did, except it was too deep for words.

'You really should address me as "Your Majesty".'

'Oh come off it Magdalen, that game is getting a bit stale.' She could have hit him but knew he was right. She sighed and tried to sit more upright in the bed but the injection had made her uncoordinated.

'As a doctor I can't really encourage you in what are clearly fantasies.'

'Not fantasies, modes of existence. I move about from one existence to another, on several planes at the same time. I am a traveller in time and space. I suppose the nearest you could get to it in your ideas would be to call it a metaphor.' He looked alert and scribbled.

'A metaphor is not an actuality.'

'To me it is. I'm very intense you know – it makes everything more real.' Dr Murgatroyd simply looked at her then, a bit puzzled and even wistful. Magdalen treated him to her most dazzling smile which scared him.

'Well my dear, the sad thing is that if only you believe in these "existences" of yours, then they rank as fantasy. That's the way the world is.'

'That's the way your world is. Not mine.'

'You are in the world – my world – I am in yours. I must repeat that if I encourage you in your fantasies then I should be failing in my job. A certain amount of humouring is necessary especially with less intelligent patients, but you are clearly not one of those.'

'You expect me to encourage you in your fantasies. You expect me to think of you as a doctor, to address you as such and so on. How do I know you aren't something entirely different on a different plane?'

'There are no different planes.' Magdalen laughed aloud as he continued, scraping together evidence of his doctorness, his name, his education, the undeniable qualities of his person. She was still laughing.

'Of course there are different planes, just because you haven't travelled consciously in them does not mean to say they don't exist. You haven't been to Tibet but you would hardly deny its existence.' He began to get a familiar look of exasperation and his rate of breathing increased slightly, of which Magdalen was aware and he was not. He put his writing pad down.

'I am afraid that in the final analysis you are quite simply outnumbered by millions to one on so many of your opinions as to the nature of reality that to an older school of psychiatry you would have been labelled "mad", and are even now in need of hospitalisation. I really do want to help you, and I'm not doing very well. I shouldn't argue with patients as you probably know, but I am trying to reason with you. Outnumbered, by millions.'

'So you always follow the majority?'

'Of course not. I judge for myself as we all must.'

'I am judging for myself.'

'But you are in no fit state to judge for yourself. I can see in your eyes that you are simply playing a game with me. Own up, you know you suffer from delusions. That much progress we have made in our past talks. We were trying to distinguish between delusion and reality, and you were making progress.'

'All the planes have their delusions, that is a great part of the difficulty of travelling in them – it takes several lifetimes of acquiring wisdom to know your way about. I am so far from perfect it is no wonder I get confused at times. You expect too much.'

'I hope not. You look sleepy, perhaps I should go now and let you rest.'

'Please don't, I'm enjoying this chat. I get very lonely in here you know with only the nurses coming and going. Most of them are very hostile.'

'That can't be true, they're trained to be friendly and kind.'

'Oh yeah!'

'You haven't been badly treated, admit that.'

'I've been made very unhappy by some of those nurses, they're bitches, and at least one of them is stark staring mad, that Gerhard is utterly crazy. She steals my clothes and other patients' clothes and dresses up in them in secret. I think I'm the only one who knows that.'

Dr Murgatroyd wrote more notes about paranoid tendencies, persecution fantasies.

'The thing is Magdalen, you are not consistent. I am always me, and yet you become other people. All that about the White House, Queen of America. There is no such thing of course – have you ever been to America? I don't believe I ever asked you that.'

'Yes. About ten years ago I spent three weeks there. I was very happy and everyone was very nice to me. I wish I could go again, I know a lovely man there called Louis Sakoian, I was in love with him but we didn't have an affair because I was married. He's been married since but got divorced although I think he's in love with somebody else now – but we're friends you know and I'd like to see him.' She had tears in her eyes to her own surprise.

'Well if you'd make an effort to get a greater grasp on the reality which we all call reality, I can bet that it will be the reality in which you could take a trip to America, money permitting, and meet him again. A change of scene would be just the thing when you are convalescing – would your husband mind?'

'I don't think so. He doesn't really care what I do.'

'That's not the way I see him. He telephones often, even visits although it is a long distance – sends you nice presents and letters. He does care very much.'

'Not in a way I call caring. He is just concerned not to have a mad wife, he doesn't want to be a Mr Rochester you see but he tries already to pretend I don't exist. Unless I conform to his idea of what I should be, he thinks there's something wrong with me.'

'A common failing – but there are degrees.'

'Ah yes. Degrees.' They sounded sinister to Magdalen. Failed degrees. Third degrees. Degree nisi – oh no, that was decree of course, but whatever was a nisi?

'If there are degrees, you should understand me much better than you claim to – or at least sympathise.'

'I do sympathise. I really do. I am trying to think of some practical approach to your problem – I know you don't care for the occupational therapy we offer here except the creative writing, but I can't help feeling that joining the pottery class would help. You are suffering from boredom.'

That was his first acute perception today, Magdalen thought – she was suffering from boredom.

'You are right, I am bored. Of course I'm sodding well bored – look at the décor in this room for a start – look at the company I'm limited to – how often do I get to go out to an art gallery, a disco, a party – think how tedious the diet is in here – if I wasn't bonkers when I came in I would be by now anyway. You kindly gave me the freedom of the place for me to walk around in but it was so boring my creative mind had to turn it into another planet, another world. I can't understand why you don't do the same – hey! why not come along with me on one of my trips, you might find it very interesting?' His mouth gaped slightly, a distant look filtered through his greenish eyes, his bow tie twitched, his earlobes reddened.

'How nice if that were possible.'

'Anything is possible.'

He wrote 'optimism indicating manic phase possible try

10mg Valium'.

As breezes carry messages a mist of unawareness passed across her outer self, and tears formed in her eyes. She could not think why.

'Now Magdalen you begin to weep. Tell me.'

'It doesn't come out in words.' What a fool he was, how could he ever help her? He was not fluid enough, he had a yardstick where he should have had a wonderful sculpture of curves in space, for each patient different.

'Come with me, it *is* possible, it *is*' – her voice became loud – 'I can show you amazing things you have never suspected.' She had somehow co-ordinated to the extent of gripping his lapels. Pulling him down to her, she shook him to stir up the sediment but he expertly grabbed her wrists, pushed her back into the effects of the injection, rang for the nurse, smiled tightly and left. She yelled after him, 'It's your great loss, not mine, you're the kind who can't reach out for life you let all your chances slip by!'

'Now then Mrs Hayward you mustn't upset yourself. Have your medicine.' Oh God our help, it was no use arguing, she swallowed it knowing it was poison. They drew the curtains miles away.

'You will soon feel a lot better, just relax.' She laughed loudly, she was relaxed, what did they know about relaxation? It was possible to cut wafer-thin slices out of the tension surrounding these people and make cucumber sandwiches.

'Oh go and fuck yourselves!'

There was no rejoinder, they left the room. She giggled at the delightful possibility that they had gone to obey her. She hoped they enjoyed it.

92

23

They had tucked her in too tightly with their paddy paws but she had been too sleepy to protest, not connected, not quite in her body. Nobody cared what she thought back home; here they cared but sometimes misconstrued. Understandably. She felt like an unread book in a forgotten corner of a library. As a child she had been able to become larger or smaller at will during childhood illnesses. Measles had enabled her to contract from being a normal six-year-old girl right back to being a baby. Could she do it now? The sheets would not be tight then. She recalled you began with your hands, feeling them very small. The technique of controlling your dreams began with seeing your own hands and recognising them while dreaming, too.

Her hands were tiny, plump and soft, rehearsing effective action, wiggling like sea anenomes. Her arms were weak. She could just raise her head from the pillow for a moment before it fell back, not supported by her infant neck. Alice in Wonderland would have understood the feeling. She kicked and squirmed and found there was plenty of room to raise her knees. That was lovely. She managed to bring one rubbery little foot into her hands and then pull it up to her mouth so she could have a good chew at her big toe. A bit like the yoga classes but without the inane voice of the teacher prattling on. The foot liked being chewed by toothless gums. Life was quite good.

The bars around the cot cast shadows on the horrible brown wallpaper. The light moved slowly through a parchment lampshade sewn with thongs to spotty wire and the fly shit on the bulb made clouds on the ceiling. If only her mother had kept that lamp it would be worth money now, with its naked female fascist being taken a walk by a police dog, all gilded. Neither dog nor woman had primary sexual characteristics; Magdalen could see through the folds and the fur to the nothings. The dog was dragging the woman off to a dark forest to rape her; they both desired it but it would remain fantasy. Magdalen moved on, two years old now. The foot chewing had been replaced by exploring between her legs for catalogue. The word 'catalogue' always made Magdalen blush; she had been smacked when they had discovered what she did, and told her that she was quite wrong: catalogue was a sort of book and not the nice smelling stuff you found between your legs. Her teddy bear had liked it too, he had snuggled down there, rubbing to cause pleasure. Sometimes the bear fell onto the floor, slipped through the bars of the cot, where earlier she had thrown her bottle when she had finished the milk. Her mother had been so proud that at only six months Magdalen had fed herself at night from a propped up bottle and 'threw away the empties', a thump on the floor heard from downstairs where they were also drinking. No cuddles while feeding, not necessary, train them to be independent right from the beginning.

Magdalen, now five feet six, glared back at the present version of a modern table lamp, a steel worm with one baleful eye. Dr Murgatroyd had told her she had constructed these memories from what she had been told.

He was not of the school which might use hypnosis to retrieve womb experiences, retrace the steps through the Valley of the Shadow to discover why a patient was so sad here in the present. It was one of their few points of agreement. Magdalen knew that she remembered, relived experiences, and knew also that no amount of retrieval of unhappy childhood days could heal them. They had, like all sad memories, to be let go of, finally. Grief held onto turned into bitter poison, corroding the heart.

To Dr Murgatroyd she was full of false memories, delusions, hallucinations, dreams and fantasy. He was stuck in one world and would not, could not enter any of hers. Her memories were real but he had been trained to discount them. She wanted a clean slate and he wanted brainwashing, and here they argued. Plenty to go at for both of them.

Sitting in a high-chair playing with mashed potato, sculpting eggs in her hands and throwing them; getting smacked when mam returned. End of art career according to some schools. Taking her first steps thinking, I can walk from here to that chair, the one with the cream and brown triangles in the plush, so she had got up and done so.

'Look! Look!' Excited parents destroying her concentration, heavy sitdown, didn't bother to try again for six months, too self-conscious. She painted and danced, she was not repressed. People in art college would get a BA for chucking mashed potato or walking from one chair to another come to that, none of that proved anything. It was no good digging up the past to heal the present, the waves of anguish were merely replayed. A kind of necrophilia. She turned over, cuddled the covers around her for now she was not quite cosy enough. Sometimes she wished she could sleep for weeks, complete and dreamless oblivion. She had argued that this was not at all a desire for death but probably an effect of tranquillisers. Whenever possible she did not take them; not all the nurses stood over her like Nazis.

'I say, are you there?'

'We are here.'

'I think I'd like an orange cut up with a spot of brown sugar on it, some brown bread and butter and a cup of Ovaltine. My mam used to give me that for supper sometimes when I could not get to sleep.'

'Certainly, but our metabolic charts of your chemical pathways indicate that this food will keep you awake, it is high energy fuel.'

'The soporific effects are psychological.' They did not comment upon that. She enjoyed the snack immensely and was almost asleep as she drained the cup. 'All gone!' she said, as part of the magic, and slipping gratefully into a lovely rest. No consciousness at all for a few hours. Not possible while still alive, probably, but there was no harm in hoping.

24

This time in Morocco she was alone. Last time she had travelled with Clive, and it had not been much fun. She thrust from her a memory of hallucinating a road going downhill when it had actually been going uphill, proved at last by stopping the car and rolling a can of soup. Heatstroke, fatigue, blood poisoning from an insect bite, and not a lot of sympathy. Now, she was heading for Fez, anticipating the orange trees, the fountains, the souks and the shade. A very beautiful city. Having stopped not long since to brew mint tea she made the last few kilometres quite fast, still mid afternoon and not yet worn out; time to find lodgings before the rapid falling of dark. The contrast between the ancient and modern parts of the city was very marked; she headed away from the modern part, she was looking for something else.

She parked the car and decided to walk around for a while, and was instantly commandeered by an Arab boy offering his services as guide. Well, why not, they were usually correct in saying that the better souks were elsewhere, away from the tourists.

'Missis come with me, I show you good souk.' He led her down narrow streets to even narrower streets and she had slight misgivings. All she needed was to finish up as a white slave. But they were in a souk where the goods were of excellent quality and the tradespeople did not importune but sat quietly making things or chatting to one another. She was the only tourist in sight, all the other women wore the tight black veil and carried large burdens or pots on their heads, not looking at Magdalen with her shorts and shirt and sunbrowned face. There was a stink of sewage and spices and cooking and rotting fruit and high meat. She noted a hand-painted sign of a freshly pulled tooth dripping blood, held in what appeared to be an ordinary pair of household pincers. What if you got a toothache here, did they have anaesthetic or did they dope you up on kif? Trip as you drip, dream as you scream. Her young guide tugged her sleeve. 'You buy fine shoes!' he urged, stopping at a sandal-maker. They were indeed very beautiful sandals. She was offered a tiny wooden seat and began trying them on. How many dirham?

The boy began bargaining for her, she supposed he had an arrangement with the sandalmaker for a percentage. A bright and lovely child. However, she knew lots of people who would immediately want to take this child and put him in school, give him school meals and the doubtful benefits of Western medicine. He was a trader, did he need to be turned into something else? Did the women in the veils need freedom? Of course they did, but try telling them that, they would not even speak to her she knew. In five hundred years perhaps there would be changes for the better. And that applied not only to Arab culture – the child interrupted her thoughts with figures and comparisons of one goatskin sandal with another.

'But I like these the best,' she told him, smiling. He shrugged, OK, and the bargain was struck with handshakes all round.

'Missis come now I show you good place.' She followed thinking, if I get robbed or lost it is my own fault, I should have noticed the way back. She felt like an alien in this place, and enjoyed the sensation. Being alien shook up her psyche and made her see everything, including herself, with fresh eyes.

The boy led her on through a doorway by a tiled well and then up what seemed to be hundreds of steps. He brought her to a ruined balcony overlooking a courtyard. How wonderful, he had taken her to where she could see into the courtyard of the mosque. Impossible to be allowed in and around downstairs of course, but from here she could see a great deal. It was all very beautiful, the tilework unbelievable. He took her around galleries to see more tiles and carvings, and then out on to a flat roof by a wonderful tower in blue and white and yellow. It glittered magically.

She stared and stared, awestruck and delighted. There was a clock with carved animal heads projecting, making shadows which worked like an elaborate sundial. Her young guide told her it was a thousand years old. Magdalen felt that she knew that already. Had she read about this? There was something strange about the whole place, an unreasonable feeling of familiarity. The sun glanced off the tower in brilliant daggers, the carved animals stared, Magdalen was entranced. She had to pull herself away again to go and look over the balcony, which was broken in places. Below was a fountain and a fig tree, and she felt fear. She had looked over this balcony before, a long time ago. Not in this life, but maybe hundreds of years ago.

Magdalen wondered if she was beginning to suffer from dehydration and decided she had better go and find a long refreshing drink in a shady place and then find a lodging. But she could only stand and remember.

She had been young and in love. She had been sold to someone else, a nasty old man with broken brown teeth and strange desires. She saw the face of her lover. Smiling, lean, dark, beautiful. She had jumped from this balcony to her death on the tiles below, by the fig tree. She saw the tiles approach as she fell. Her guide tugged at her sleeve.

'Missis come back you something wrong.' She stepped back just in time before she fainted, pulled backwards down a tunnel in time.

25

Clive had escaped college an hour early for lunch again, having become distressed at the cyclic nature of his thoughts. Anger at Magdalen for not letting him know where she was. Fear that she might be in some real trouble. Worry that he could not keep up with the workload because he was becoming bored with it. Guilt because he knew he was drinking too much. Disgust at himself because he knew he was beginning to fit into the archetypal college tutor who judged the female students as much for their breasts as their brains. Justification because who would not in his position. Ah-ah-h! He could *throw* something. He still hadn't bought any vitamin B; he kept meaning to.

By the time other tutors and students began to filter into the bar Clive had had two pints of excellent bitter. It was during the third that he began to feel more relaxed, more human. Everyone had problems, there was no point in driving yourself insane over everything. The world really began to shape up in fact. It was wonderful what a good old English institution such as beer could do to your *weltanschauung*. It made a world of difference.

26

There was a flowering cherry of deepest pink outside the window of Magdalen's room. As she packed the last of her things she paused often to look at it, thinking, it would bloom just as I decide to leave. Japanese print images in her mind she packed with care, folding and rolling even though most of the clothes were not the kind which minded a few creases. The window was open and birds sang in the tree. Her departure was more resembling the end of a pleasant holiday in a nice hotel than an escape from what had become a concentration camp. It seemed that whatever decisions she made, irony was in pursuit to change the lighting effects.

They had strongly advised her to stay. Naturally they would advise her to stay at the prices they were charging. Mental illness had its class system as much as anything else – crazed and rich was better than crazed and poor – and she would soon be poor if she stayed here. She needed her savings and few small investments for more important things than being sick. She was not sick. She had simply needed to be away from White House and Clive and all that for a long think and a rest. It was a great pity that she had been treated with various drugs, it had held back her thinking and feeling for far too long a time. Next time she felt like cracking up she would go to a Greek island, money permitting, and swim and explore and rest. Such things should be on the National Health in a real civilisation; in the end it would cost much less.

She intended to travel before returning to White House to

discuss anything with Clive. She felt very strongly that if she contacted him then everything would fall apart again. He argued too much and she became tired and agreed. He would want them to make (yet another) fresh start. She did not feel ready for that, doubted that she would ever be so but did not rule it out. The longer she stayed away from him the less she missed him. What that meant she did not know. In leaving this place she was following what she chose to call her instincts, and felt so strongly that even though she had no plans in particular, she was doing the right thing.

Her packing done and details checked (there was an après-ski suit in ghastly colours which did not belong to her so she left it hanging in the cupboard) she took her bags down to the reception. The clerk had all her papers and asked Magdalen to sign several things. Magdalen asked to read everything before she signed it and the clerk looked very offended and her look showed clearly that this attention to detail was a sign that Magdalen was unwell.

'I'd like to take them outside to read them, it's such a lovely spring day.' Without waiting for permission, leaving her bags as security, she negotiated the thick glass doors which were an optical joke pretending to be two ugly ungraspable knobs floating in air, and walked down the gravel drive. A left turn took her among willows to a small gazebo. All the trees were beautiful, full of blossoms or buds and many kinds of leaf and birdsong. A lilac promised such a heavy flowering that it was almost worth waiting a further ten days for the heavenly smell.

When she left this place she would go where there was a lilac tree in bloom. Perhaps she would go to Edinburgh and walk around the Botanical Gardens. She had loved Edinburgh! Clive would never suspect she might be there for he knew her to be a person who always headed south. An image of Clive frantically searching Kew Gardens while she was calmly in Edinburgh's Botanical Gardens amused her very much.

She must collect her car from where she had left it for overhaul before coming in here. Clive knew it was there – was he going to play at detectives? He didn't have time, this was the busiest part of the academic year. She read the papers. She saw nothing alarming and set off back to the reception hall. As she approached the drive her heart almost stopped at the sight of Clive parking their Rover and walking towards the reception hall briskly. He was carrying flowers and a polythene bag.

She scuttered back to the shelter of the gazebo, sweat prickling and mouth dry with fear. Why had he come here today, unannounced? It was midweek, he should be busy. It was about four hours to his work and their home. What was he playing at? Had the staff here alerted him? Good God – very probably – the lousy bastards! She was being *humoured*! Treated like a prisoner. Well, she knew what to do about *that*. Escape, as planned. All her money and cheque book with the bags in the hall. Christ! Act cool. Snoop. Clive could possibly be taken within the building to confer with Dr Murgatroyd, that would be her chance.

She was almost up to the glass doors again, approaching at an angle in the hope of not being observed, when she realised she had left the papers in the gazebo. If she was caught it would make her look even sillier not to have them in her hand. Running, sweating, she regained the gazebo and gathered up the papers which had fluttered about. Once more the sidewise approach to the front door; peer in. Deserted. Swiftly she entered, put the papers on the desk, got her handbag and two smaller bags, left the valise and fled again, running as fast as possible this time down the drive for the main gate. Were they watching her, was she observed? Dr Murgatroyd's office overlooked the main drive but, from where his desk was, seated persons could not see anything much from the window. It depended upon whether or not he was in a pacing mood, for then he often went to the window to look out, back turned to a patient or, in this case, Clive.

The main road outside was deserted, a country road not very much used. Telephone box half a mile away, too far to go with the luggage. Not as strong as she should be; being weak enough to go into a hospital, one became even more weak. Magdalen hurled her bags into the ditch in among a lot of ferns and brambles, covered them over and fled for the call-box at her top speed, praying every moment that her absence had not been noted.

The call-box was occupied by a woman telling her entire life story to some deeply interested listener. Eventually Magdalen ordered a cab, thinking quickly that it would be better to ask it to pick her up outside the front drive so that she did not have to ask a cab driver to stop while she got her luggage out of a ditch. It looked like strange behaviour. By the time she had raced back up the road, retrieved her luggage and was standing trying to get her breath she realised that this too looked odd; usually people had cabs from right outside the front door – there was no other point of reference to be seen. And any moment a nurse or a doctor or Clive might come and see her. Dreadful minutes.

The cab arrived, the driver showed no sign of any interest in her at all, then she realised that she did not know where she was going.

But of course, go and get her own car. Where? She couldn't think, it seemed so long ago. Flustered. Collect self.

'My car. I have my car in a garage – I seem to have mislaid their card, one moment.' She rummaged and found it – all was well. She reminded herself that she was not after all a criminal, that she was not hurting anyone – except possibly Clive who would be angry and frantic at her disappearance – sat back and had a smoke.

Fortunately the driver was not the talkative kind; Magdalen did not wish to swap life stories with anyone until she had sorted out a few thoughts, acclimatised to 'normal' existence. Taciturn, he drove as if playing starships in overdrive and so they arrived at the garage with a stylish squeal of tyres. Ten percent tip seemed to be what a normal woman would give. He did not spit.

The bill for the overhaul was exorbitant, and she had to believe that the filter had needed changing, the oil, two new tyres and an electrical fault detecting. How could she prove otherwise now – on her arrival she had not felt up to checking everything herself, had only been aware that the car behaved in a peculiar manner. Cutting out, skidding, things like that. For a panicked minute she could not find her bank card but then things shaped up, she paid, filled up and left, mentally tossing an imaginary coin for which way to turn. She did not want to leave any tracks and so forebore asking for directions. She finished up in a nasty looking little market town but there were motorway signs so did not finish up but left without even stopping for what would have been stewed tea and stale 'home-baked' scones.

On the motorway her strength returned. It had to, there were so many competitive lorries.

It was a long drive but she stopped only for more fuel, hating plastic cafés and their plastic food. In Edinburgh at last she found a promising pub, got a room and showered, changed, and only then went down to the bar to contemplate the dinner menu.

After her third long cold delicious Ricard she decided two things. That she would have a really good meal, beginning with smoked salmon, continuing with a large rare steak of Scottish beef with french fries and salad, and ending with various bits of cheese and some strawberries. Her other decision was that she was not, nor had she ever been, and this was final and inarguable, mad in any way.

All that had given that impression was that her experiences were not common, and that Clive was envious of her and therefore frightened by her.

There was a further decision, but she was not yet ready for that.

27

Abel Murgatroyd, trained psychiatrist, expert amateur Chinese historian, pragmatist and atheist ran into the foyer of Twelve Trees giving the appearance of his hair standing on end and his eyes on stalks. The receptionist prevented herself from noticing anything amiss. Dr Murgatroyd had been through a difficult hour, they all had. Mrs Hayward had disappeared without either signing her discharge papers or paying her account, her husband had arrived minutes later and there had been consternation to say the least. But Dr Murgatroyd did not look like this because of all that, surely? She had seen him stage managing Mr Hayward out of the building by one elbow, smiling, concerned, rumbling voice of reassurance – so what was going on? He did not tell her. He ran past and went to his consulting room, locked the door behind him and went to throw himself down on his couch.

He had seen it. It had all happened. He had experienced an hallucination. He was terrified. When the trembling stopped he went to get himself a very large gin and tonic but it tasted foul. He drank it rather fast anyway. What the bloody hell was going on? His phone rang, he switched it off. His other phone rang; he ripped it out of the wall like they do in movies.

He tried taking long slow deep breaths but they would not come even, his throat closed upon the square chunks of air most painfully – he understood now how some of his patients felt experiencing 'psychosomatic' choking fits or being drowned in air. Terrible. He lay back and began to get himself together. He got up and walked around and fell to pieces again.

Whichever way you looked at it, he thought desperately, whether it was an objective phenomenon, an hallucination or a practical joke (he had seriously entertained that possibility for almost a whole minute), it was significant. He was not a Jungian, he had early been disabused of all that nonsense by excellent tutors. He paid quite a lot of mind to Freud, admitting his narrow scope; he respected Adler and found him eternally practical and applicable; he was gradually becoming more and more of a behaviourist, noting that human beings are as easily trained as dogs, act and react according to influence. Brain chemistry fascinated him. Religion did not fascinate him, mysticism made him nauseous. When he read books they were novels about real life, he could not stomach fantasy, science fiction nor Dennis Wheatley.

But he had just seen a flying saucer.

The utterly peculiar roaring buzz of it still rang in his head. The powerful smell of ozone still stung his nostrils. The beautiful unearthly coloured glow of its incandescence was still visible to his inner eye. It always would be.

What the hell was going on?

Sucking comfortingly on a large cigar interspersed with slurps of further alcohol he became aware of his other more normal self talking alongside his irrational self. They were having an argument. Behind those two voices in him there was something else. It told him that perhaps it did not matter whether the experience had been 'real' in any sense he was accustomed to, the fact was that he had experienced it, and had enjoyed it very much. It had been beautiful, he had felt physically elated, sort of sexually excited all the way through, awestruck, full of joy and wonder. It couldn't be bad, but of course he would soon experience a reaction, his patients always did after their visions – by God that was it! Jesus shit!

Somebody had spiked his morning coffee with some foul poisonous drug! How lousy, how stupid, someone would suffer for this! He leapt up to the telephone to call an instant meeting but it wasn't connected any more, he blathered into a bit of plastic with a bit of cord hanging off one end. Shit. Christ. Damn.

Which drug? And of course, he had heard himself revealing what part of him thought about his medicines. It was possibly a typical lysergic acid experience, but never having experimented he didn't really know. They hadn't any of that in the lab. It had been twenty years since they had tried huge doses upon obsessives – another flash in the psychiatric pan, no good at all.

The humming sound, look up, see a great glowing ellipse. Hovering, descending. Landed on the gravel drive very slowly. A circular door had opened, apparently making a kind of music as it did so.

From his right, running down the path from the gazebo, Magdalen Hayward had gone straight up to the thing. The door had emitted a beam of awful white-violet light, sort of encasing her, she had floated up it, disappeared. The whole show had ascended vertically again and then very rapidly zoomed off to a nothing dot, leaving behind a ghastly emptiness. Just like those goddam Third Encounter movies as far as he knew – he never went to things like that, they were not interesting.

Someone knocked on the door. He looked around for evidence of insanity, put his glass in his filing cabinet and went to open the door. One of the older long-term patients, an old chap who had somehow become the gardener, stood there, an ecstatic smile upon his face.

'What is it Toddy? I'm very busy just now.'

'Dr Murgatroyd, I've seen it again. That's the third time, I didn't mention it before, I forgot you see. But this time I remembered, I tried to remember and I did.'

He looked for approval, he had trouble recalling things and the doctor was always pleased when he could.

'Oh splendid Toddy. What then?'

'I saw this spaceship come down and bear up that lovely woman in J ward. I always knew she was something special, now they came for her. I call that grand. It's very important, I know it is.'

'Yes Toddy. It is grand, it really is. I'm very pleased indeed. Is that all that happend?'

'More or less. Only trouble is, it spoilt the gravel. I'd just got it all freshly raked and now it's gone and burnt a damn great circle all black and nasty. And some of the flowers as 'ad it too I fear to say. I'll be needing a say so to get some more bedding plants if you want it looking nice.'

'Well you shall. Ask my secretary. You can put in whatever plants you think right, lots of them.' A look of true pleasure toned up the old face, anticipating the delight of doing the flowerbeds all over again.

Abel Murgatroyd and Toddy walked together out to the front drive to inspect the damage. Toddy was saying that the salvias had been excellent in a local nursery last week when he'd gone for the pansies.

The awful thing was that when they got to the scene of the incident, there was no sign whatsoever of any disturbance in either the gravel or the flowers. They both searched diligently, two sets of hopes being horribly dashed. Abel had hardly been containing his excitement and terror at the prospect of confirmation of something utterly abnormal for it was what he deeply desired.

'Well I'm terribly sorry Toddy but you seem to have made a mistake.' Tears formed in the man's eyes.

'I saw it. I saw it.'

'I'm sure you are telling the truth. But the fact is, the flowers are just fine. Tell you what, you can go and get some new plants anyway, and put them where you like.' It seemed to help. Already the old man's vision was fading, he had so many, it didn't stun him into eternal awareness the way it did Abel Murgatroyd – for that is what he felt, that this experience somehow marked a turning point in his life. Two people had seen it at the same time, perhaps there were others, like Jung said, a symbol of wholeness had arrived from the collective unconscious, a projection from inner space. It was easier to swallow than outer space anyway.

Thank goodness his vacation was due at the end of the week, he could not talk to patients yet, he would not feel right.

He decided to explain the damaged telephone by saying he had tripped over it; he had thought to blame it on an angered patient but now that seemed mean and nasty.

28

Clive strolled around the gardens of White House as darkness slowly came, changing shapes and transforming colour. The magnolia was his favourite and he looked up through its black branches, savouring a really good bit of grass spiked with a smidgeon of resin. He was really getting into this smoking thing, even though he had said he would give it up. It eased one at the end of a harrowing day and yet had none of the nasty side effects and destructive properties of alcohol. He felt a little bit guilty smoking alone as he always had when drinking alone, but reasoned himself out of it by asking himself why one should not experience pleasure when alone: it was merely an extension of Christian (and come to that Buddhist and Hindu and Moslem and Jewish) terror of spilling seed on the ground. How foolish. This magnolia with its pure white cups bloomed for him alone, he was in love with its perfection.

He listened to the cicadas for a long while before it dawned upon him that there are no cicadas in England. There must be something wrong with the telegraph wires. The sound increased in volume until he could hear it in his bones. He was transfixed, holding the roach which went dark, its life burned out. The night had come and yet the sky was lit up with a weird violet glow. Clive experienced pure terror and found it more like pleasure. His mouth fell open. The magnolia tree spoke to him in a foreign language and he longed to know the message. His bodily presence in the universe became more real than he had ever imagined, his whole flesh vibrated as if an orgasm had spread through every cell. His questioning reasoning mind fell asleep and did not ask what the hell was happening, or it would have stated 'epilepsy – stroke – heart attack – diabetic coma – sudden onset of hidden disease – overdose of powerful herb – nervous breakdown'. Perhaps his reasoning mind dreamed these various conclusions but it was so far away it allowed him to experience simply without analysis. Clive felt to be levitating; it was utterly delightful. The magnolia began to make sense, what it was saying was a message from Magdalen.

'I've gone away for a while to think things through, I'm OK so don't panic, sorry but I can't talk with you yet or say where I am, also I forgot to pay the bill I'll straighten with you later.' End of message. In her voice, coming loud and clear through the magnolia. Marvellous. His reasoning mind came close for a while to suggest that it would be a very good thing if everyone spoke through magnolias, one would not get a magnolia bill quarterly.

The light in the sky formed itself into an elliptical shape overhead. A beam directed itself towards Clive. He put up his arms in welcome, he had been waiting for this all his life without knowing. The beam dissolved him into itself and he ascended vertically into utter black unknowingness.

29

Louis Sakoian waited for Magdalen Hayward in his favourite downtown bar. What a woman! Very weird, she could be described as very weird. But not a fake, not a pseud. She stared through her eyes and through your eyes, it was not chilling or spooky, it was a convincing form of communication.

She was so naive. She truly believed that here in New York she could come to no harm because she meant no harm and did not invite harm. God! She would not listen to his stories of muggings, they meant nothing to her. He must protect her whenever possible. He didn't know her very well, he was a friend of a friend but there had been a mutual attraction and he had been taking her out and around during her visit. She would only be in New York another week and then she had to get back to her husband. She said she loved him and was always faithful. That was a bummer but he had to respect it, and anyway he didn't really want an affair. Wasn't ready yet, not after the Charlene thing. Hell. He ordered himself another sherry out of the wood and then Magdalen arrived and asked for a pint of beer. She looked totally stunning to him with her strange mousy silk hair piled up into a knot, her silk shirt, elegant pants and high heels. Lipstick and mascara even, she didn't often do those things. When she smiled he almost fell off his bar stool, and began blathering something about his day at the office, explaining how he came to be wearing a scarlet pirate scarf around his forehead – he always kept a change of personality in his briefcase. She laughed loudly and heads turned and stayed turned. He felt proud, nobody in this bar had as weird a woman as this, although they must all be thinking that she was merely attractive but too loud: they didn't hear her talk about her head and what went on inside there.

'I had a great day today, there was a parade in Fifth Avenue, all Puerto Ricans protesting, and this Nazi came up to me and said he thought that Hitler should have won the war!' She pealed out laughing, could he imagine, there really were people like that! Yes, he could imagine all too well, he knew that there were people like that, he'd met them too. Horrible.

'I'm so hungry, I didn't eat today, I forgot.'

Louis could never forget to eat; being six foot six tall and built like a wrestler perhaps helped his huge appetite and love of food.

'Well I thought I'd take you to a favourite place of mine called the Mistral. Very good French cooking, you'll love it.' She knew she would.

The waiter at the Mistral obviously thought highly of his dinner companion and paid their table a lot of attention. They ordered pigeons done in red wine with mushrooms and olives, and had a good Burgundy with them. As the drink disappeared she became noticeably higher, and although the waiter still paid attention with fresh napkins, moving the flowers out of the way of her flailing hands and other details, he looked slightly alarmed. Louis prayed that she would not do something really stupid; much as he liked this woman he was not yet past the stage of being able to swallow all embarrassment at a female companion taking stage centre and doing something silly.

She picked up bits of pigeon and sucked the bones, enjoying everything, lustily wiping fingers and mouth and then setting to again on a wing or a leg. Louis thought what the hell and followed suit, congratulating himself on his cool. The meat was good after all, why waste any?

Magdalen asked for more garlic in the dressing for the salad and it was whisked away and brought back refreshed accordingly.

'Marvellous!' she said gesticulating. 'Absolutely marvellous.

I adore garlic.' Louis ate some too, depending upon the principle that garlic for two meant no odour for either, for maybe he would kiss this woman later, her love for her husband notwithstanding.

They got to choosing another course and mutually decided upon fruit salad in Kirsch, a dangerous choice for when they said Kirsch they meant Kirsch and not a few drops in the juice. The dish was heavenly, the fruit tasted as if just freshly picked. She gazed at him in ecstasy. Does she like sex as much as she likes food, he wondered absently, not asking the same question of himself. Magdalen was thinking similar thoughts. She thought, the best sex I've ever had is a thousand times better than any food, but if you can't get sex then by golly food is the best thing in the world. She didn't worry about her figure, it stayed bone thin whatever she ate.

Louis and Magdalen talked about books during the meal, comparing likes and dislikes, comparing judgements, found much in common and also many favourites which the other had neither read nor even heard of. They made notes on dinner napkins and Louis had to pay for them to take away for they were damask not paper.

They ate Brie and Stilton, delighting in the very good coffee, the feeling of intense companionship.

'I've never felt so close to a man so quickly, I think men and women should be friends but you know usually men only think of women in terms of sex and other services, if you see what I mean.'

'I don't see why one should not have both in a relationship.'

'Neither do I but it's a funny thing, when love comes in friendship goes out, I've noticed this.' She was thinking of Clive who had been a good friend, once.

'Well that's really sad Magdalen, I hope it isn't quite true.' They finished their meal and left. He took a cab, suggesting that they go on to a nightclub. She was delighted – a nightclub – in New York – how marvellous!

She was so easy to please, like a well brought up child, unbelievably delighted at everything.

He took her up Radio Black and they had cocktails opposite the Empire State, their table placed so that it seemed to be floating in space.

'I think this is amazing. I've never seen anything so beautiful. Look at the Empire State, the way the lights go, you know, it looks like a great spaceship coming in to land. It has come a long way and now it's landing right before us. So beautiful it's like a dream.' With anyone else Louis knew he would be cringing at the sheer corn, but he knew that with her it was true, it was exactly what she did think and feel. He felt it too.

'The inside of my head is like that when I'm high, it lights up in a thousand colours always changing, a vast computer.' He could have kissed her there and then but his mind told him not to attract even more attention. People were staring, not now because she spoke loudly but because she seemed to be so transported her face glowed, she radiated happiness. He touched her hand. It was enough, too much. And also, two drinks was plenty.

Outside they took another cab and then walked over the Brooklyn bridge which was quiet. She said she felt like jumping off and swimming; he felt fear. He had dropped a tiny bit of acid before this date and told her so now, somehow her words reminded him of that.

'Really! I thought you shouldn't go out when you'd done that. I've never tried it, I don't think I dare, it sounds so dangerous.'

'It's not dangerous but I'm sure you just don't need anything like that. You feel like a very together person to me, you don't need things like that.' She fell silent and shy, flattered and disappointed. Someday perhaps she would try something like that, but he should know – funny thing though, he seemed no different to normal.

'I don't understand really – do you feel a lot different, aren't you tripping?'

'Not very far out. I only had a little, it sharpens the perceptions.'

'So really, we aren't in the same world are we?' She sounded so sad and lonely all of a sudden.

'Of course we are. I feel it very strongly and so do you. Maybe the acid was no good, really, I guess we are both high for the same reason. A good night out.'

'I'm sure you are right.' She didn't sound convinced. He hated the acid he had swallowed. Wished he had not mentioned it – it was true he had forgotten it, he was not tripping. But when they took another cab it seemed that suddenly, she was.

They passed a bank with an amazing display of plastic flowers and she stole one in full view of a cop. Louis' heart sank as she danced up to the cop.

'Please officer, accept this token of my regard. I think you New York policemen are wonderful.' This was it; arrest. He wondered how to get rid of the other half tab of acid which he foolishly still had in his wallet.

'Why thanks ma'am, that's really nice.' The cop put the flower in his belt, lacking a buttonhole, and wished her a pleasant visit to New York. Louis said nothing as they walked along, she more dancing than walking, taking a few Fred Astaire trips up steps and Ginger Rogers swings right down again tapping in her high heels. He sweated secretly and was still delighted, scared.

There were people on the street but not many. Down and outs, scurrying men, couples like themselves. He never recalled afterwards how it happened, but there she was on the steps of the Guggenheim Museum, giving a speech to what at first was a small group which grew into a small crowd. A speech. At one thirty in the morning. In New York City. Louis watched fascinated, having made a feeble attempt to drag her away into the safety of a cab.

'It will be all right,' she had said, looking into his eyes with that clear stare which hypnotised.

'When I regain power and am Queen of this country in the White House once more, I shall proceed to right as many wrongs as possible, starting with the worst injustices that can be found. There will be no capital punishment, for when peace and love reign there will be no murder nor rape. No good person wishes to commit such crimes, and in a country where everyone is properly fed and housed, all will strive towards goodness.' Louis felt a pit of nausea, on the one hand because she was spouting utter bullshit, and on the other because he was now genuinely frightened for her. She would be taken to a cell, deemed barmy, drugged, imprisoned – but it was not so. The crowd began to cheer, agree, yea say, much as they would have done at a religious revival. The crowd consisted of drunks, tramps, cripples, two cops standing with mouths open, hookers, a couple of male gays with arms around one another, bleached hair and lipstick on one, tattoo conspicuous on the other, a Chinese with hands up wide sleeves possibly concealing an axe, heroin addicts with ruined flesh and other people not so easy to typecast. And himself, Louis Sakoian, unfortunate escort of a dangerous lady. The acid in his bloodstream told him that she was right, beautiful, good. His bloodstream told him, as it metabolised the rest of the acid, that in future he would be extremely careful who he took out to dinner, and that he must be more dominant afterwards and keep himself out of trouble. But was this trouble?

It was weird. Nobody was heckling or throwing things, spitting or jeering. The cops who should have been moving her on or inside just gazed as they listened. She had constructed her own surreal world and invited everyone else inside and they had accepted. Weird. The city had fallen silent, all those few on the street were here, the traffic had stopped and the breeze was stilled, only her voice moved.

'We are to have a cleaner America, free from pollution so that when you have children their brains will not be damaged by lead poisoning, insect killers and effluents. Half the depressions that people experience are because industrial shit disturbs their brain chemistry. You will be able to eat healthy food again and know it contains goodness, and not sneaky poisons in among the good whole wheat and the shining oranges. You'll be able to eat a tuna fish sandwich without wondering if it's full of cadmium and you won't want to smoke yourselves into cancer and emphysema because you'll be more relaxed and not nervous all the time. There won't be continual noise drowning what you say and making you feel irritable. I'm going to show people how bad noise is by showing them silence and music and friendship talk instead, then we won't have to enforce by law. We'll realise these things in good sense and out of a desire for harmony. All the races will forget about hatred, the ghettoes will be a thing of history, they won't be needed any more because those who value their culture can continue that culture anywhere and everywhere, creating interest in other races rather than hostility. My new America will show the world how to live, we shall then truly be the Promised Land, and the pursuit of happiness will no longer be such a tough rat race where whenever you find some happiness you are too damn tired to appreciate it.'

The crowd laughed here. She would have made quite a good stand up comic, thought Louis, laughing also.

'And something else I want and you want because it's only sensible is to stop all this nonsense about the two sexes. In a good world people won't argue about who needs most money, who's the breadwinner, who's most intelligent, who should and shouldn't have or not have the right to education and a career and have rules as to how to dress and how to look and whom to sleep with and when. Love will rise where it arises and not within some convenient marriage which kills that love and makes a prison out of a home. There are many sexes in this world, and to persecute everybody except those who conform to male and female with only two roles to act out is barbaric. You people know that, I know that. I want everyone to know it, to know what is in their hearts and admit that this famous pursuit of happiness includes male and female homosexuals and also if two people of different skin colour love each other, they have that right. Love is hard enough without making more problems.'

The crowd laughed again and Louis saw tears roll down the face of the gay with the tattooed arm. Any other time he would have looked away and cancelled out the memory but now he almost felt like saying something nice in order to help. Magdalen was going on about old people, how senility was largely due to wrong feeding, wrong living, and that old people had a right to work and to be in the community until they died if they wanted to, and not be hidden away in places were they would die of boredom and misery, looked after by strangers.

There was a clash as something flew through the air and Louis leapt but it was OK. Somebody had thrown a razor on the steps at Magdalen's feet. She was talking about war and killing and how it would be a thing of the past because when the earth had been inherited by everybody and there was no overcrowding nor religious persecution there would be no reason to declare war. Louis fought with his cynicism, thinking, you aren't talking about the human race my lady friend, you are talking about a race that will never exist, and all these ideal thoughts of yours are fit only for a pubescent angel. She was sillier than any flower power maniac had ever been, she was so silly they were listening and understanding. She had not only naivety but a true innocence which attracted and spoke to the deepest hidden half-dead or paralysed hopes of every person in the world. These down and outs and night rubbish people were closer to real hopes, having been taken further from them than a well-fed healthy secure middle-class white American could ever imagine except in some unreal self-induced neurosis expensively indulged in by twice weekly analysis.

Louis watched something too amazing. A Chinese turned and looked up at a huge black man and put out his hands. They embraced. Chinese were the most racially prejudiced of anyone and also the most prejudiced about homosexuality. They were the least friendly, the most impenetrable. Louis felt a strange trembling like a fever coming on. Shock. Emotional shock. He admitted it, he agreed with what Magdalen was saying, she was right, and everyone else surely wanted all this peace and love and happiness too? How to accomplish it? She made it seem possible. Others felt the same, the example had been set and Irish embraced Puerto Rican and black embraced cripple and cop embraced drug addict and woman and man and all kinds embraced and threw down guns, knives, coshes in an obscene pile on the steps.

This was a magical night. Her face radiated love and peace and goodness.

Then there was the wail of cop cars approaching like demons in the air. Louis saw the flashing lights and knew they were homing in on the scene. Somebody was a traitor, a judas had gone to report a riot at the Guggenheim. Chaos as the first car drew up, the sight of Magdalen unperturbed, ready to explain everything to the wonderful American police. Oh no, that was too much. He exerted his ordinary sense and strength, grabbed her and made her run with him, turning up and down the blocks until they found a cab. He gave his own address in Chinatown. She didn't speak or argue but sat back in the corner, trembling violently.

They had six flights of stairs to climb to his little pad but they made it eventually, both breathing hard and sweating. She sat on the bed with its pale grey cover, in the middle of his bachelor mess of musical instruments, books, dust and used crockery. He made coffee and she took some black and after a while looked up into his face.

'I love you, Louis.' He felt ill and bitter. He wanted her, but how could it happen? Even to kiss her would be to take advantage. To make love now would be like desecration, afterwards they would wake up in a world where every possible bad thing happened, including Louis Sakoian taking advantage of a naive and crazy English wife of some man he'd never meet, a destroyed marriage, a one off fuck that should have been a bond of love and friendship to last forever.

'I love you too Magdalen. Let's get to sleep now, I've got to get to work in the morning by eight thirty. Have you got the cab fare back to West 88th?' She checked, she had, she was quite practical.

Exhaustion lay like a blanket on their pain and when she awoke in the morning, Louis Sakoian had gone. Magdalen did not weep or plot or plan, but thought, well, Clive wouldn't mind any of this really, how could he? What hurt Clive was the idea of sex with another man, and she had never had that. Perhaps never would. Not find out if love could endure and passion

120

flourish and sex lead to higher and higher states of ecstasy. Magdalen searched for an earring in the covers, found it and put it back in her lobe without looking for a mirror. Louis Sakoian. How strange a thing love was, how unsought these feelings had been. How long would it take to die? Was there a way to crush it like a beetle or would it fade thin from starvation, have hallucinations and be turned to something else in the mind, a great passion that never existed?

She withdrew all her feelings back into herself, knotted them up in love-knots in her centre, grasped upon the pain.

'Martyrdom, denial, celibacy, unfulfilment, loneliness, a cross to bear, something to endure. I hope it makes me grow, is good for the soul as I was told, because I feel that what is really going to happen is that it will destroy me. Perhaps it's what is destroying the world. All that imprisoned love, it turns to poison.'

But what else could she do with it? She could not find an answer. One thing was certain, going to an evening class in pottery, as Clive had suggested, was simply not enough.

30

Three weeks had passed since Abel Murgatroyd had experienced his vision. His entire life had changed, and would change more. Any psychiatrist who sat here as he was doing, telling the matron of his outfit that ECT and drug therapy were evil, and that he had been told this on the highest authority, which is to say by the voice of Raphael the angel in Aziluth of Yesod, branch of the Kabbalah Tree of Life, was doomed to have his life changed. He didn't care, he burned with religious fervour, with certain knowledge, nothing could shake that.

'Well Doctor, I'm sure you are convinced of this, but I can't simply stop all the patient's medication in the middle of courses, you must realise that some of them will have epileptic fits, go into depressions, commit suicide etc etc. One can't simply withdraw therapy suddenly, don't you agree?' She was waiting for Drs Manning and MacIntosh to arrive, they would deal with it. She was deeply distressed that this should happen here. She had been very happy working with Dr Murgatroyd. Everything had been very orderly under him, he had a very tidy mind. Now, it seemed to have gone wrong, he must have been overworking – she did not like the sneaking suspicion at the back of her mind that he had thrown up a psychosis. It was not for her to decide although of course she often did. Matron played a quiet little game of first-to-diagnose-correctly; she usually won.

'Doctor, I know I'm stepping above myself to say this, but I do think you have been overworking. A rest might be a very good idea, even the strongest of us needs that as I am sure you will agree.' Abel thought, I may be tired but that couldn't possibly cause all these wonderful visions. He slept about seven hours a night which was plenty. He didn't drink a great deal. He ate a balanced diet. Matron must think he was deluded.

'I may be overtired Matron, but I am not suffering from delusions.' How often the patients said that. He reflected sadly upon how frustrated they must feel when disbelieved. He vowed to listen more carefully, not to dismiss the fantastic so lightly. When you had experienced the fantastic, everything changed.

'Do you not have a vacation due?' she asked.

'Not for six weeks, Venice this year. I couldn't possibly take time off now, in my absence so much damage would be done to my patients. I can't allow drugs and I must rescind several decisions for brain surgery. I'm very much afraid that most modern therapy is not only useless, it's wicked.' He looked sadly at the floor and she hardly knew where to look.

'Our patients must be treated, that is why they need to come here. We have a very high success rate. And with what would we replace our therapy, might I ask?' She had forgotten her place in her indignation. What was the fool proposing to do, let all the raving loonies run around free?

'Matron. The mad are not mad, they are enlightened.'

She did not answer, there was nothing she could say aloud that would not be rude, and she could see no point in arguing. He would be in therapy himself very soon, that much was clear.

'The truth is, Matron, and I do not expect you to accept this just as I put it to you but I do beg you to consider it – "reality" as we know it is only one of several realities, all parallel you see, in a sort of spiral. It is possible to move from one to another, indeed it should be normal but we are all asleep, tricked out of our birthright by an unfortunate gene which keeps us in a state of unknowingness. This is only my way of trying to interpret this truth of course, others have done it much better and why didn't I read more carefully when I came across such references? Asleep you see. But once the scales have fallen from the eyes the whole world changes.' He knew he wasn't making much sense to her, he really ought to shut up but he couldn't. Ever since the first vision he had felt increasingly excited, ideas had kept pouring in, voices, visions, dreams, just like the descriptions in the Bible – Matron probably thought he had religious mania. Perhaps he had, perhaps this was it. His objective mind told him he was a religious maniac. But the other part of him told him he was a privileged repository of truth and that, come what may, it was his duty to tell people about it, to attempt to open their eyes.

'Well then Doctor, if there are several realities, which of them is "normal"? How does one distinguish?'

Matron was actually listening, he had made a breakthrough. She had asked an intelligent question.

'None of them, that is the point of what I am saying. What you and I have agreed upon as reality is only one of many. If they are all realities, then they are all equally important. This is how a person can travel in both time and space, don't you see?' She was saved from further time and space filling by the entry of Dr Forbes.

'Manning can't come, MacIntosh will be here in a moment,' he said to Matron, not acknowledging Abel first as was the custom. It was this sign which told Abel that he was in trouble. He was a patient. They had come to get him. To 'help' him as they would put it to him; he could imagine their patronising tone now. Panic gripped him by the balls. He must get out. One shot of a sedative and they would have him in bed in a locked room in no time.

'Ah, hello Abel, how are you?'

'Not too bad. A little overtired perhaps. I'm just off on vacation as a matter of fact. Cab's waiting I think.' He got up and left the room and began to run. There was no cab, it was pure ad lib. MacIntosh was approaching.

'Hello old chap, can't stop, cab waiting.' He ran very fast, the squash club had done him good after all. He got in his car and drove off like Starsky and Hutch, not even looking in his mirror to see if he was followed. He wouldn't be, those chaps were both slow thinkers. By the time they'd worked out what was happening he'd be miles away. Never to return. It was the only way. If he stayed to save the patients he would become one. He must go and think, hole up somewhere and get a plan together as to what to do with all his new knowledge.

Meditate. Meditate upon what it all meant. That was it, that was what meditation was for, possibly. He'd never given any attention to that sort of thing but now it seemed real. Could one drink while meditating? He hoped so fervently, because it was opening time, and this called for a quiet place. He knew a little country pub about five miles away that would do fine.

What he needed to do was to get something on paper, a kind of manifesto, a record or something.

The barmaid at *The Goat* gave him a big smile when he came in.

'Well I must say you look well today, come up on the pools have you?' She drew his pint of perfect Guinness very slowly, leaving it to top up as she cut him his customary ham sandwich.

'Skip the sandwich Aileen, I'm on a diet. I've gone vegetarian as from today. You look well too I must say. No. Not the pools. Quite the opposite in a way. I've just resigned from my post and I'm going to write a manifesto.' Aileen stared. Why? Just as other people were losing their jobs, he chucked his in. He must have caught something from one of his loonies. The poor sod had lost his marbles.

31

'We would like to make an experiment with you.' She jumped. She had been miles away, dreaming that she was walking up a mountain in Wales in daffodil time. She was bored and needed exercise and real fresh air, not this stuff they made for her. She hoped they meant that they wanted to experiment alongside her, and not use her for an experiment. They had not tampered with her spinal fluids yet, or anything else physical, but they might.

'It is the question of a male companion. We are very interested in this question of human sex.' Masters and Johnson in space. Go on.

'It would seem that you have certain powers in what you call your imagination. Perhaps you would like to have the male of your choice. If it is in the known universe then we could give this to you as we give you your environment and food.' Now they were talking.

'A great idea. You mean, right here in this room my "order" will appear? But it takes a while to have a relationship form.'

'You will cover that in your picturing, we will create accordingly.' Brilliant. How could she do that? Invent a recent history so that she and the – it – already knew one another. 'He' would be in a state of shock if he suddenly appeared in a room on another planet, so she must think of something to encompass two realities. Normal enough for a sexual relationship to develop.

'If I don't get it right and I don't like it, will you promise to elide it and bring me safely back to this here and now? I can't handle an inharmonious relationship at this time, I don't need it.'

'Certainly. As always, we have your welfare in mind.'

So, what were her fantasies? A really loving, tender, intelligent, well-educated man who would treat her as an equal. Somebody who knew enough about sexual energies and female anatomy and chemistry to make love making magical in every sense of the word. Good looking. Stylish. Not bigoted or chauvinist in any way at all. What turned her on? Black. Dreadlocks. It was the equivalent of a male's dumb blonde, unworthy. But whatever she asked for it would be a figment, in a manner of speaking. Was there a black man in the known universe who had all the other qualities she desired? Was there a man at all with such qualities? How could they meet and then naturally progress to a sexual relationship?

'Could you sort of temporarily put a lot of people into the environment, I need background for this.'

'Yes if it is within reason.' Hm.

'OK then, my experimenters, start taking notes now about human behaviour and this female's fantasy. Although to be honest I don't really think this could happen. But experiments sometimes fail.'

'True. What do you have in mind?

'Hold tight, my aliens. We are going to a party.'

She had managed to get them refreshing drinks with ice, no mean feat in this crowded room. If she wasn't careful she would be drunk and, considering the nature of the experiment, that was not desirable. Too much drink ruined sex; some was OK to overcome residual inhibitions.

'Cheers.' They clinked glasses, hers almost spilling. She felt rather nervous, how did he feel? He seemed to be very relaxed but of course that could be a front, the one which all people put on at parties, until they really were enjoying themselves. They had been discussing the business of her floating consciousness and he appeared to take everything she said as being perfectly normal.

'Yes, I've always been like this to an extent, but smoking and tripping helped to remind me even more. And meditating. I've done Tantra yoga and a few Kabbalah practical exercises. Sufi too but that was ages ago.' Magdalen looked at him in disbelief, he was so beautiful. Very dark skin, almost black, and thousands of little rough knotty plaits that he called dreadlocks. All his clothes were black too, the only lights the flash of his marvellous teeth, his three gold earrings and his eyes. And a large ring on his right hand, second finger. Silver, with a Yin Yang symbol.

'There's a real strong Sufi outfit right here in Edinburgh, I was in that myself. It's quite a power trip believe me, you can get a long way with that but I think they misuse it if you follow me. You know?'

'What, influencing other people you mean?'

'Sure. And things. Corrupt as they come some of those teachers, use the energy of the students.'

'But I always thought that was the way that Sufi students paid the teacher for the knowledge.'

'It's one thing to give but it's another to have something stolen. I know somebody made very ill by that, the teacher just drained them.'

'What really? That's a kind of vampirism. How?'

'Well first he got this young woman to fall in love with him and then he fed off that energy, took it right off her spine after it had got up to her heart.'

'Isn't that what all men do to women?' The young man looked at her with respect and interest.

'Well yes, could be – but giving isn't stealing. Like I said. If they made love like I want to with you then that wouldn't happen.'

'What would happen?'

'They'd exchange energy, and that would multiply and make a new energy for both of them.' Magdalen blushed. He had put into words her thoughts about what love should be, what should happen. She had thought it was a lonely theory. She gave him a quick smile of encouragement but had to look away out of shyness. His eyes were so bold but it was not unpleasant. She looked around the party.

He'd brought her here after she'd met him in a pub. She had found a rather drab little room with a gas ring, and a shower in a cupboard, clean enough and fairly cheap. Her money would have to stretch, she couldn't stay in expensive places forever, she wasn't a tourist. The room was very brightly lit with one central bulb in a pale green shade and she had found this depressing to sit reading under, so she had gone out for a drink. It seemed like years since she had done anything so simple.

Once, she had gone round to the local with Clive quite often, for 'the last drink', but those evenings had ended in bickering and she had given them up. He had gone alone. To go by herself had seemed impossible, but times had changed – or she had. In the pub she had ordered a brandy and turned around to find a seat. She had seen this beautiful person sitting there watching her and, without considering how improper it might seem, gone to join him at his table.

'May I sit here?' she had asked.

'I'll be one disappointed man if you don't.' Just like that. Clive would have called it a pick up, so would her mother, with much disgust. Never mind that.

He took hold of her hand very gently. His skin was very warm and dry. She could feel electricity. The music was very loud, reggae of a sort she hadn't heard before. A lot of rhythms, clever dubbing, not much vocal. Much better than most on the radio. Compelling her to dance. He had asked her if she wanted to come to this party and she had accepted without considering. She hadn't been to a party for what seemed like years either; the college parties with just the staff were very dull, and the staff-student parties to which wives sometimes went were painful. They made her feel as if she did not exist, but was that faceless nameless being of no account, a staff wife. She had at first watched Clive dancing with the young girls without any negative emotion, but had gradually realised that she was being made a fool of by them. She had asked a youth to dance and got on well with him but Clive had been funny about it afterwards.

She had given up going to those parties, she felt unwanted.

Here, with all these young people, she did not have those spooky feelings. She had been accepted. Anyone who wanted to come to this party was accepted. There were a lot of black people, some of the men with Rasta hair, some shaven close, the women very reserved and elegant when black; drunk, outgoing and in all kinds of dress when white. There were three older people, one an obvious leftover hippie with masses of grey hair, long beard, patched jeans and beads. The other two were also male but dressed in the current style with short hair and sharp shoes, one pair expensive white kid. A mix of factory, college, rebel and underground. Very nice. The air was thick with dope and cigarettes and pipes were passed round often. Plenty of wine too, and a table with delicious looking health salads and wholemeal bread.

Magdalen was on a high. Why the hell hadn't she come here before? She answered herself. Because of the intertwining of time and space a thing only happened when it happened, no other time or space. She laughed at her own circular glibness, knew it for truth. She fitted in here, older than most, younger than three, it was of no account. She felt an affinity with this man sitting by her. He spoke and she had to ask what he said.

'I said, we haven't found out each other's names.'

'Magdalen.'

'Mary Magdalen?' She blushed. She hated that, at school she had got it, Clive had used it at first until she had burst out angry in tears one day. The role didn't suit her, although she had been cast in it. To wash the feet, be body slave, and not the consort, the lover, for such a one – what morbid thoughts. But let it go, she wanted away from all that sickness, digging up the past, ghosts. Now was OK, wasn't it?

'Just Magdalen, no more no less. And you?'

'Royston. I don't really like it but I didn't decide on anything better yet. If I get into this outfit we're starting I'll change before we print a record label. I'm a drummer.' Magdalen was very impressed.

'Wow! Reggae?'

'Reggae, jazz, voodoo. All at once.' He smiled and suddenly leaned forward and kissed her cheek. Just touching him was exciting. Kundalini people were always a thousand times more exciting than anyone else, she had been kissed by two. One a teacher in the Tantra group, which was why she had left because Clive would never have understood that ritual *maithuna* was anything but adultery. The other had been a Sufi student who had kissed her after a dancing meditation, causing her to leave her body on the instant and trip off to a heaven with him for several months or years, while they stood there for not more than a minute earth time. Kundalini. Very powerful thing once awakened. She knew that Royston had it awake, knew how to use it. Even ordinary sex would have been good with him, she felt that intuitively. Ritual sex would be something so unbelievable – it was in that part of her which she kept locked. She was breathing deeply.

'Maybe tomorrow, without drink or smoke, you might feel like making love with me?' He gazed into her eye, her third eye.

'Yes.' There was no other answer. But there might be problems. Better be brave and mention them now.

'Well I really mean yes and I hope you still will, but there's the pregnancy problem and also the disease thing. I'm paranoid about that last and I've nothing for the first. You see, my husband had a vasectomy at a time when I thought we both – but anyway, I don't know.' She had trailed off like a teenager, her throat choked with the thought of how Clive had cheated her out of children. He'd wanted that vasectomy for his mistresses, he didn't want children and he'd persuaded her that she didn't either, saying, the two of us is all we need, a child would intrude.

'I swear I'm clean. And we can make it a real *maithuna*, no emission, very slight risk. Get a spermicide for the slight risk.' So that was settled. Magdalen thought of how people would feel horrified at the 'no emission' bit, feel sorry for them both at the outdated holding back technique, but they didn't know that it wasn't going to be frustrating. An orgasm held back on purpose is an entirely different thing from an orgasm not reached or denied. So different that the Sufis, the Taoists and the Tantras have used it for millennia as a means of reaching the outer limits of human ecstasy. Transformation of energy. The rocket fuel for seventh heaven. St Theresa could do it by herself, Magdalen had done it accidentally by herself – it would be quicker and better with two. She grasped her Shiva's hand for when Shakti finds him, there is to be no denial.

32

Miriam pulled the covers up over her naked body for in Clive's bedroom it was cold, even in late May. She lit two cigarettes and passed him one.

'Gee thanks Lauren.'

'For you anything, Humph.' But did it have to be cocksucking? She didn't really like it and had gone to the bathroom to gargle with his Listermint afterwards. These middle-aged guys weren't always up to it, very disappointing. Now he wanted to talk. Heigh-ho.

'I still can't work out what actually happened. It was very weird and it's getting weirder.'

'Replays. Mushrooms do that sometimes, it's good. I don't know what you're worried about, it isn't keeping you from your job or anything. A few dreams and visions are good for you – some people never have such things, you're lucky. I expect you're worried about going bananas like your wife.' Not that any wife of his wouldn't go bananas after a while.

'A replay. Hmmm. It's like catching malaria, it returns when the conditions are right.'

'Well you've got that exactly right. Just so. Once you've seen through the top layers, you can't pull a curtain down upon it. Your inner eye is opening, that's very good. And then again, maybe it isn't the drug, maybe it is like a virus, maybe you caught it off your wife and the mushrooms just feed the virus.' This preposterous idea made Clive snort and put out his cigarette. He drank some of their white wine which was now tepid.

'What rubbish. You will turn out to be a science fiction writer if you are not careful.'

'Well why not?' He didn't ask if she referred to becoming a writer, or was still on about her little theory. The minds of women were not only lateral, they shot off in all directions. Miriam pulled his hair, something which he hated, and told him, 'The way I see it is that it is perfectly possible to have a foothold in several realities.'

'Oh Christ. You haven't been reading Husserl again have you?'

'Yes. I do the required reading as well.'

'If it creeps into your essays you will lose a good degree.'

'I'll get a good degree, I know how to perjure myself.'

'Miriam, I really think . . .' She tugged his hair again.

'Shut up Clive, come on, let's do it my way this time.'

He didn't like being bossed around in bed, he wasn't used to it and didn't want to get used to it. It was all very well women's rights and so on, but some women, once you got them going, it was like taking the lid off Pandora's Box and finding it full of porn videos in which one was an unwilling actor.

'Later Miriam. I need a shower and something to eat.'

'You need a course of Ginseng. I'll do it myself, you can watch if you like.'

He blushed fiercely. She had hit upon one of his deepest fantasies. Nothing on earth would get him to act it out. He felt a pang of nostalgia for Magdalen at her most inhibited, the way she sometimes actually hid under the bedclothes.

'Oh all *right* Clive, go and have a shower, I was only kidding.' As he left the room she reached for her bag and got out her copy of *The Eagle's Gift*. If Clive knew she was reading Castaneda he'd have a fit.

Well, let him.

33

Royston propped Magdalen up with pillows and gave her the hot drink. She had influenza rather badly. She had slept three nights in his flat after the party and then started to feel very peculiar. This was a shame because their ritual love had been what is quite rightly known as out of this world, and it made them both feel so good that they should never have had any bad luck or sickness again. But they were back in this world with its flu bugs – so far Royston hadn't gone under. He made a wonderful nurse, unlike any other man Magdalen had met or heard of, anywhere.

'I'd better tell you about this drink. It's a West Indian flu remedy – you didn't know we got flu in da West Indies did ya? – what I do I steep a lotta ganga leaves in rum for three weeks, then mix a large shot of that in with some hot water, lemon juice and honey. Kinda hot toddy with balls.' Magdalen managed a croaky laugh and accepted it gratefully. Just in case he should get the flu, Royston took a precautionary cupful himself.

'Royston, you're marvellous.'

'Keep talking.' She would have liked to have said 'Royston I love you' but not only did those words scare her, she didn't know what they meant. It was a conditioned response to sex and kindness from the opposite sex. Love was a dreadful tricky word. He'd said it to her several times but it stuck in her throat. Better not to name things, sometimes. She just smiled at him.

'Good drink?' he asked.

'Divine. I shan't know if I've got the flu or I'm tripping.'

'That's the idea. Beats Beechams any day.' He got one of his books and a notebook, sitting up to the table near the bed. He was studying medicine at Edinburgh, in his fourth year. He was a mature student aged twenty-seven. He had been a factory worker but had done nightclasses and saved, got a place and a grant. He was not wasting it, he had worked for the privilege of more work. Magdalen was awestruck at his determination, comparing it unfavourably with the way her husband's students wasted their time, having had their chance to study handed to them on a middle-class plate, the effort of gaining A levels having been their worst hurdle. She had worked at art college, very hard, but done the idiotic thing of getting married before her finals, and moving away as Clive changed jobs. Too late to go back, too late. Royston thought not, they had discussed all that. Perhaps he was right, but she wasn't ready for that yet. She had to learn to survive.

She watched him work, eyes down, moving from the text to the notebook. He got up twice to refer to another book on the shelf, and then again to put on a tape of U-Roy.

'You don't mind music?' he asked her. Of course not, but didn't it disturb his work? Of course not. The music and the drink soothed her aches and shivers and she began to look around the room dreamily. Anatomy charts, posters of black musicians, an advertisement for a meeting of the National Front with additions in felt-tip pen, notably 'Good Ole Ozzie. memo polish jackboots'.

'I've got to go tomorrow, I'm sure I'll be well enough. I can't stay here forever.'

'I don't suppose you can. Hope I'll be seeing you again.'

'I hope so too. But the room I took, they'll think I've disappeared.'

'How long you planning on staying in Edinburgh?'

'I hadn't any plans. I'm sort of floating, trying to think what to do, where to go. Sort things out.'

'Will your husband be looking for you?'

'I don't know, maybe. But I can't see him yet, I just can't. I shan't know what to say, and he'll start taking over my life again. He'll say that my disappearing is a sign that I'm not ready to leave the hospital yet. But I feel better already, except for the flu. I can't sleep well sometimes, but those pills do all kinds of things you know. I don't want any more of those, no matter what.'

'I hope my future patients aren't as awkward as you – what could I do without medication today?'

'Be a new kind of doctor. Study acupuncture, diet, get your patients to meditate, things like that. Vitamins, group disc-ussions, orgone boxes – only use antibiotics as a last resort.' She could see it working.

'I'd never get on a register in order to be struck off immediately. I'm not going to be much use going back to Africa to cure leprosy with witchcraft, am I?'

'I didn't know you'd ever been to Africa.'

'I haven't, literally. But I'm heading there, not as a Haile Selassie freak, but as a trained medic. They need them.'

'But white people are now giving more credence to African medicine, herbs, witchcraft and so on.'

'Sure sure.'

'But Royston, you *know* about Kundalini, how powerful it is. You *know* about herbs – this brew is very good stuff, I'll be better tomorrow.'

'I think I need my medical degree as well. People who get into healing hands and herbs finish up being cranks even if they did have something real.'

'What would you do if a female patient came to you with depression, pre-menstrual tension, dysmenorrhoea?'

'Diuretics, maybe vitamin B6, tranks if that doesn't help.'

'But Royston, you know that's wrong. That woman would be suffering from an energy block due to insufficient sex and real orgasms and being sexually rejected when menstruating.'

'Yes honey I know that – but what if her husband just ain't about to co-operate – do I help out personally?'

'Yes please.'

'But you don't have any of those problems do you?'

'Actually yes. Although I don't mind so much since I saw

through what was happening. If I could get it together to go to the bathroom I think I'm bleeding.'

'Come on then, I'll help you.' She was bleeding.

'Oh dear, it's so embarrassing.'

'Not embarrassing, Magdalen. Divine.'

34

Magdalen walked around the garden at White House, a hot sweating English July tea time, that time of day not easily comprehended by Americans. She was looking at the flowers, remarking their progress and nipping off a few dead heads, tying up, pulling out cheeky weeds. Playing, in fact, at being an English lady. Trug and all.

It had not been too dry but there had been plenty of sun, an unusual combination which did not require her to battle with aphids. The roses were glorious, and as she picked off dead heads she spoke to the bushes, expressing praise and gratitude. She had once felt a complete fool talking to plants, but after practice and seeing the results given by encouraged plants, would not have minded being overheard by however mocking an intruder.

'You see, I told you that seaweed fertiliser would make you feel strong. It's very good stuff, anything from the sea is, even if you don't think it natural, being a land creature yourself. I'm a land creature, and I eat seaweed. I do a lovely Japanese kind called Arame with onions and soya sauce and vegetable stock, and sometimes also lemon juice and chilli – wouldn't suit you done that way, but the extract seems to be fine for your temperament. Do keep flowering, it's worth it, you look so beautiful.' Plants who were not spoken to and loved and encouraged found life a great struggle. Magdalen knew this from experience and always paid special attention to a plant which sulked. Sulks were not childish tantrums but a symptom of a lack.

'Bleeding hearts, sad name, fading already, but don't despair, I'll see you again next year.' The shrivelled pink bells nodded in a rare breath of air exhaled from an invisible mouth. A hot sigh of longing on a lonely afternoon. Bees too sleepy to spread pollen, flowers wondering how to masturbate.

The nasturtiums roared like tigers, invaded Magdalen's eyes with brave attempts at mustard gas bombs, begged to have the caterpillars picked off.

'Oh all right then, but you know, if you host these caterpillars they do turn into butterflies, you can afford a few, you've got too many leaves anyway.' Magdalen always found that the exotic tropical colours of nasturtiums excited her, she could not stop looking into their sexy hollows, feeling blood in her cheeks. One iris out, just one. Dignified, too proud to say it needed a damper spot.

'I'll transplant in the autumn, I'll get some proper peat for you – I've never tried irises before, I'm really sorry but I can't know everything.' The iris stared at her reproachfully, prayed for rain. The flower was a yellow specimen, and Magdalen bent down to look closely. Apparently she liked butter and alchemist's gold. Fool, thought the iris, smiling.

The sky was darker, dust-devils played at the edges of the paths, put motes into her gold-filled eyes and grit between her bare toes. Perhaps it was getting cooler – how nice to have rain. The tops of the lilacs, blooming rather late, danced foolishly, not knowing that one good storm would see them off. The sky threatened rapidly, and it was not cooler. It had become the kind of afternoon when, if Bette Davis had been better understood, dreadful murders could have been avoided. But she rolled her eyes in the days before the invention of the negative ion machine, and long before Masters and Johnson.

Magdalen muttered to herself about cutting some roses for the table – there were plenty to spare. Her secateurs were in the trug. Six red, two pink, three orange and yellow mix and one perfect white. What a perfect, faultless, immaculate, sweet-smelling, half-opened white, still attached. She held its branch hesitating to cut. There was a flash of mauve lightning, startling her. A thorn pierced her thumb, ouch! The white rose recoiled too, not thinking like Magdalen, that she must hurry and put things tidy before the rain. The trowel, the box of weeds, the plant ties – always lost bundles of plant ties, most annoying. Oh dear, it would have been nice to have tea outside today, hoping for butterflies, ten to three, which kind of honey for God's sake, makes all the difference to me if not Rupert Brooke.

And the string. Dots of hot rain like old shillings from Heaven, darkening the pale stones, bits of sky falling. The birds stopped singing, huddled apprehensively out of sight, plenty of foliage to shelter them, they hoped. Stones did nothing, let their dust be wet, and earth opened its mouth gratefully at last at last, water. Not much though, and hot. A crack of thunder shook Magdalen into action, very loud bang and roll, quite near, too near. The hair on her neck prickled as she thrust things in among the spiders and cracked plant pots wishing for the thousandth time that Clive would clear out the shed. Men! Good at smoking and contemplating in gardens, and not for much else.

A vicious shaft of energy hit the path right in front of her sizzling into the new wet with a stink like hot bleach and dogsfart. She screeched and swept up the trug of roses and scuttled indoors sweating. God! Another foot and she'd have been a cinder for sure. She filled a pail with water taking care not to touch just in case lightning could come through a stream of tap water – but how silly – and immersed her roses for a soak. No white rose. She could see how the arrangement would not look right. She so wanted a white rose, it was necessary. But it was dangerous out there. No, it was not, she chided herself for a fool even as the house shook with loud energy and the electric light flickered down and up as if some poor bastard had climbed the pylon to die in style. People didn't get struck by lightning, not in their own gardens. What about all the other people outside, hurrying home, out of all those would she be chosen? Of course not.

She had to get the secateurs from the gloomy shed, and something nasty crawled along her arm. She flicked it off, not to be deterred. Secateurs in hand, Magdalen ran.

The trees were lurid in their verdigris, a super-green with more life than sunlit green, glowing underwater colour reflected from the sun which had dived into the earth for shelter, too bright to be extinguished, furious at not being more powerful than cloud. Strong sky, powerful metal sky, gonging together its breasts and buttocks at the command of other fires.

The rose was there waiting, the best one on that bush. Blindingly white, the brightest light, it had absorbed the lightning, it hurt her eyes. Its petals were exquisitely new and smooth, almost invisible veins throbbing in anticipation of the deluge. Magdalen took the stem in her hand, admiring the flush of bloody colour in the thorn and leaf, decided where best to snip. The secateurs chewed instead of biting; bending the stem she grasped in haste again and on the thorn. Again, a cut, more successful, almost cut, secateurs just about kaput oh *damn*, but she could not tug, must cut. As the steel functioned, finally severing, in her ears sounded a shrill keening wail which jarred her skull, shot pains through her teeth and made golden hairs stand up on her arms like needles. The rose thrashed in her grasp, wriggling, her blood dropped onto its virginity and from its very heart that rose screamed in agony, pausing for breath to scream again cursing her as she stared into its erect stamens revealed as it curled back its petals in a sneer of vengeful loathing. The rose screamed at her atrocity and its terrible sound was hardly drowned by the rolling thunder shaking the stones upon which Magdalen crouched, frozen. The water fell solid to wake her from the ghastly trance and she got herself into the kitchen kicking the door fast behind her, sobbing now with fear, tears in rivers.

She swore repentance, she had not realised, she was full of pity, washed off the red blood and the green, tore herself upon its thorn like a demented nun and found it the best vase to itself, was quite distraught. But it was too late, the murder was done, the rose whispered that she could not atone, was cursed, and from that white creature there slipped a whiter wraith of a rose, upwards floating and luminous in the storm darkened room from which all light left. It had become Magdalen's inner world; ghost ascending, her flesh falling into the flood seeping under the door.

It was a long time after; night had come and she woke wet through in cleaner air washed by the storm and the birds were settled once more – hadn't she heard them sing?

The door-sill needed attention, the kitchen was awash. The rose, where was that? Only one thing to do, get everything tidied. Was it safe to switch on the light? She groped her way about to the bathroom to change, finding all well, got busy with a mop, functioning but feeling strange. Not only strange but rather euphoric. No point in suffering blame, self-hatred, excessive sorrow. No help at all, she could see that. Had it really happened? No, how could that be? A vision? A fit?

Eventually, at half past eleven at night, she had the place about dried, a pot of tea made and the rose in its vase on the table. The other roses were arranged in a lustre jug. Magdalen took the white rose and put it with the others. It did not comment. So that was all right. It was the sort of incident best kept to herself; as it was it might mean something, but told to Clive or a doctor it would quickly be translated into a symptom. And she had plenty of those.

Hells bells, being alive was a symptom, it was just that they did not know what the disease was, yet. What harm if a rose screamed; it had been a terrible thing, she still shivered at the remembered sound. She could choose between roses with unearthly voices and human pain, or a symbol of something meaningful in her own psyche. Either way it was preferable to being told she was epileptic, schizophrenic or whatever the latest thing they came up with might be. Hysterical perhaps? In a deep sense of the word that was certain; her womb did not wander up into her brain, but it was not only empty – no no, it was not even a biological child wish even, it was more important. She wanted love, real physical love. Not words, promises, ideas, but the real thing. She wanted again to shudder into the bliss which comes from a place that is both animal and spiritual. And there was no help, there was no lover. She screamed inwardly, the longing built up to a great storm, that was the reason: denial.

Well never mind. At least, thought Magdalen as she went very slowly to her empty bed, I have novel ways of enduring my deprivations and trials. Better a screaming bloody rose than Librium, any day.

35

'Come in,' said Royston Hartwell, flicking back his magnificent dreadlocks. The nurse showed in a new patient, a young woman.

'This is Miriam Goldsmith,' the nurse told him, smiling through blue china chippings. The nurse left and almost simultaneously they said, 'Wow! I love your hair!' Miriam's hair was a violet electric shock. Royston thought that anyone who had the nerve to go around looking like that couldn't have much wrong with them. Miriam thought that anyone with such beautiful Rasta hair was probably a musician or a dancer rather than a psychiatrist. Psychiatrists by definition were stuffy deskish types. Like Clive.

She looked around his consulting room. Marvellous. African artifacts including what were possibly a bunch of dried fingers; aspidistras, spider plants, avocadoes partially obscuring mandalas; pre-Raphaelite pictures, Persian miniatures, Paisley wallpaper, Indian rugs, Peruvian weavings; some wonderfully rude Tantra paintings torn out of library books. Incense holder, Tarot cards, I Ching. What kind of psych was this? Laing influence perhaps? She spotted a row of pipes and a king size pack of skins. Hmm.

They stared at one another. He thought, 'What problems could she possibly have? Probably frigid, a frequent torment of beautiful women, who suffered from too quickly inflamed lovers, greedy and insensitive.' She had wonderful eyes, but guarded. She did not speak so he coughed, offered her a cigarette. Choice of Gitanes or No 6, he could tell a lot from a person's choice, or so he believed.

'Thanks,' she said, taking a Gitane to his relief.

'I suppose you must have a problem or you would not have consulted me.'

'True. Shall I tell you what it is? You'll never believe me.'

'I shall have to believe that you believe it at any rate – there could be no point in your telling me a totally fabricated problem. Only a really crazy person would pay large fees to have a non existent problem analysed.' She folded up laughing with him, a bit more relaxed.

'Well –' she began but he interrupted.

'Lie down – patients always lie down in psychiatrist movies, it is supposed to relax you.' She gave him a flirtatious roll of her beautiful eyes and went to fling herself in among the cushions, making herself comfortable at great length, including asking for an ashtray. She coughed and giggled.

'Well, this isn't the centre of the thing, but it is important. I keep having strange dreams and they are a great bother to me. You see, I'm in love with a man who doesn't love me any more, and it's rather taken the meaning out of life. Whenever I ponder about things, deeply you know, I find that only one thing is really worth having.'

Royston didn't prompt so after a short silence she told him what that one thing was.

'Sexual intercourse with the man I love.' He took in this information, and thought sadly, oh dear, I think she's right, there really is nothing as good as loving sex, everybody of any worth knows that really. Oh dear, and she couldn't have that, so all else was empty.

'Yes. You are probably right. The thing is, if you can't have that just now, how to manage your feelings.' She raised her head astonished, as if he had said something really wise. Compared to her last psych it was wise, for he had tried to reason her out of her 'obsession'. Yuk.

'Exactly. But of course that's not all. I'm not actually

spending time weeping and that sort of thing, I'm getting on with my work you know.'

'You sound very confident and strong. It sounds as if it's one of those "matter of time" things, what do you say?'

'Time. Ah well now, that's it.' Mmm, she thought. Time. 'Time. The dreams which trouble me. I dream that there is no time, I don't mean, run out of time, I mean, that I'm in a timeless state and that I shall remain there forever except that even "forever" means nothing in a timeless place – it frightens me. And also . . .' She fished for a tissue in her bag, she was crying after all.

'And also, I dream that I'm somebody else.' Oh heck, alter ego, archetypes, complexes, all that. Here we go – heigh-ho. Well, it was all money.

'How interesting. Anyone in particular?' He didn't expect it when she told him that she dreamed that she was her ex-lover's wife. She seemed too certain of herself to want to become some other focus in her lover's life. But top show was nothing, everyone knew that, not just analysts!

'Very unusual. Tell me more.'

'The dreams are the super-real kind, the sort where when I wake up, ordinary life is more like a dream than the dream, until after breakfast sometimes.'

'What do you have for breakfast?' he asked irrelevantly. He was picturing having breakfast with her after a night of sex.

'Orange juice, coffee, toast, eggs, yoghourt.' He could imagine the morning sun shining through her hair as she sat with her back to the window, hunched, waking.

'I see. Tell me more about the dream.'

'And sometimes stewed fruit. I am this woman in a very comprehensive way – I have her memories and experiences and none of my own. I never refer to myself as Miriam in the dreams, I wouldn't know how. Do you know what I mean?'

'I think so.' He didn't know, he tried to imagine.

'Yes. You see, the queer thing is, myself, I never eat breakfast. But I've started getting into that kind of breakfast thing, it's now so natural when I shop – my fridge is stocked for *her*. Too.'

Gentle streams of tears running down into her ears, out of them, onto the clean pillow. No effort to stem them, as if she didn't know she wept. Her voice was steady, puzzled. Detached.

'I'm not dismissing what you say as fantasy when I say what I've next got to say. Which is, have you a very vivid imagination?'

'Yes. Possibly. But when I imagine things, it isn't like this. This is like another reality.'

'Is this other person – well – what sort of person is she?'

'She's OK I guess. Means well, gets things wrong, sort of easily deceived, duped. Very unhappy sometimes, but she is genuinely trying to get herself sorted out. I can feel a sort of anguish in her that she is trying to sort of deal with. Like dissolve, you know? I'm talking now as if I was her, but when it's happening, it's me. Really me. I would say in that case, if I was her, I'd say, "I've never really been happy except one glorious time when I first married Clive, then life was bliss. But I found out later that during that time he was screwing a young student, and so in retrospect everything caved in, wasn't real any more. Fool's paradise. My task is, to get rid of those memories, somehow convert them into life currency." She thinks like that, I don't use terms like that. She thinks things like, "There must be a better state of being than this." And then she sort of floats off into a different if not better state of being. She's like plastic or something, I don't mean plastic material I mean she moves and reshapes – that's it – she changes her shape. Or goes elsewhere. Not escaping, just like trying on new clothes. She's very strong, she's very good, centrally I mean, very. Full of love, but quite often gets herself ripped off, gets things stolen from her – not objects; acts, feelings, energy. She feels that she needs to close up somewhere, get herself mended. Oh God, I'm not making sense.' Well, she was, very much; he had to let her see that.

'You are to me. It makes sense. More – tell me.'

'Well,' and Miriam had to sit up to blow her nose. The impossibility of blowing the nose when weeping lying down has ruined many a pre-Raphaelite scene.

'The truly awful thing is, I really don't love Clive any more.'

'Who?' Pause. Her husband.

'So what is her name?'

'Magdalen.' He knew. He felt her, coming through the fabric of this younger, shock-haired gorgeous girl. Magdalen was in the room with him. She had left his flat in Edinburgh six years ago and he had not seen her since, and he always remembered. Where was Magdalen? That woman. Older, not like this. But he'd never been closer to anyone, for a short while.

'I ought to suggest that this is your imagination, again, strongly. But I can't very well.' She seemed not to hear.

'In a way it's in my head, or it is now, but not when it's happening. It's like being possessed perhaps?'

'Perhaps.'

'She's also quite crazy at times, believes weird things. Like being the Queen of America, lives in the White House and things like that.' Miriam's voice had trailed off and her eyes closed. She seemed asleep, but was still talking very quietly in a monotone.

'I think I shall invest you with a royal decree to be my psychiatrist. You will be given a badge and will be obtainable to me at any time of day or night.'

'Thank you very much Your Majesty.' Silence. Then she very slowly got up, hardly opening her eyes. She fumbled in her handbag.

'Here.' She gestured imperiously. Royston approached tentatively, and then, ceremoniously, Miriam pinned a badge on his lapel. It read 'Vote for Snoopy'.

He roared laughing and she snapped out of it, saw what she had done and laughed too.

'Now you'll think I'm crazy.'

'I certainly do. Listen Miriam, how long is it since you last saw this woman's husband?'

'Three weeks and two days.' Love measured exactly.

Had Magdalen gone back to Clive after all then? Or what? What was possible? None of this, obviously, and yet; and yet; the answer would be: he had temporarily tripped out into his own future.

'Miriam, what year is it?' She looked at him with sarcasm.

'I'm going home now to think things out a bit. Maybe you should do the same.' She was soon gone without his attempt to stop her; he could think of nothing to say, but waited for her to be gone so he could check the year. It wasn't years since he had seen Magdalen, it was a few weeks. He had been a student. What was all this office and practice stuff? A dream. Nothing but that. The door slammed loudly, realistically. Magdalen, all this is somehow your fault. He called and called aloud, desperate.

He awoke in her arms.

36

'It's really strange the way the psych just left like that without them even collecting for a leaving present. When my Dad retired they collected and gave him a leaving present it was a silver tray with some words written on it sort of scratched what you call engraved you know they always do that.' Kev was polishing his shoes, something he did as often and as thoroughly as possible. His Dad had told him when Kev had been a lad, forty odd years before, that if you had clean shoes with a nice shine then you could hold your head up and be proud no matter what anyone else said. Kev was speaking to Toddy who was a good listener.

'I'm not too keen on the new one I think he has less understanding even than Dr Murgatroyd really and when I asked Matron if Dr Murgatroyd was coming back then she told me to mind my own business she was covering up you can always tell and she's a bitch she wouldn't tell the truth even if she knew it I don't think.' He spat on the polish and rubbed vigorously. The shoes were black leather, pointed toes. He never wore them, they were his best.

'Whatever the truth is it must be embarrassing. Thank goodness I'm leaving soon. Just two more nights and then my Mum is fetching me, I'm going to a rehabilitation centre for a while, just days you know then I'm getting a job. A real job, I think I'll look for something to do with shoes.' Kev had a slight lisp and gestures which unthinking people would call 'effeminate'. Toddy watched the polishing and took in the news of

Kev's leaving with no envy and a large pinch of salt. Toddy was leaving also, and would not return again as before. Kev was never out for long, they always brought him back. Kev said it was his Mum's fault, she never listened to what he said or what the Doctor said, and things went wrong again. Poor Kev, everyone knew that there weren't enough jobs nowadays for 'them' never mind 'us'.

Kev said, 'And I miss Magdalen too, I think it was cruel of her to just leave without saying goodbye after we'd been such good friends. But I know really there must be a reason for her to have done that, you could trust her, maybe she ran away I don't blame her and I hope she doesn't have to come back. If you ask me there was nothing wrong with her, it was that husband of hers he didn't understand her and he should have been in for treatment lots of husbands do that to wives they call it gaslighting I saw a play about that once she was gaslighted was Magdalen so he could go off with other women. My Dad did that to my Mum, and me. I hate him.'

Toddy looked as if he was going to cry. His mother had gaslighted him too, had him put in here when he was thirteen and whenever he went home something always went wrong and he got sent back and it was because his mother told lies about him, she didn't love him, she had never wanted him, she loved the dog better than himself. But this time he wasn't going back to her, he was going to look for Magdalen. He'd been told to in a dream, she was a very important person, he meant to go and offer her his services, he would do anything. The question was, whether or not to tell Kev about this. He felt that not telling would be a lie. It was difficult to tell the difference between a lie and a secret. Every time he had a secret his mother had found out and called him a rotten little liar. Well, never mind her, she could go to hell.

Kev said, 'Magdalen understood what you were saying even when you couldn't put it into proper words, sometimes she understood what I was meaning even when I didn't speak although I expect you think that's just silly. She told me that everyone said she suffered from delusions, like getting out of her body and going to other places, well, I've always been able to do that but I didn't tell anyone except you, and then I told her that I could do it too so she said, well, don't tell Dr Murgatroyd or any of these people, well I just laughed because I wouldn't be so stupid. I never tell things like that, almost everybody doesn't understand. You understand don't you Toddy?'

'Yes.' That had decided it, he must tell Kev of his plan because they already had one large shared secret, so it would be a lie not to tell – and anyway, Kev might like to come too.

'I'm going to find Magdalen, I'm not going home. I could work for her maybe.'

Kev stopped polishing. 'Could I come too?' He didn't want to go 'home'.

'Yes. We could go together. I think I know where she lives, and the house is called White House and it has a magnolia tree in the garden, it shouldn't be hard to find.'

'But she might not be there.'

'We'll have to risk that. If she isn't, then perhaps her husband knows where she is.'

'Bet he doesn't.'

'Do you think she'll want us?'

'I don't know. I think so.' So that was decided. They would seek out Magdalen, it must be the right thing to do because they had both thought about it. Kev felt guilty at not saying that he had thought of it too but not told Toddy. He would have eventually though, he told Toddy everything in the end. That was what friends were for.

'My cousin Dermott came to me last night,' Kev said, polishing again. Toddy's eyebrows went up. Cousin Dermott was a ghost, part of the reason that Kev kept on being sent back here. Dermott had been dead for twenty-five years but he kept coming to Kev with advice.

'What did he say?'

'Well, don't be cross, I was going to tell you, but he told me to go and find Magdalen, and to follow her. Like as if she was a religious leader sort of thing.' Toddy gawped. Crikey! That was something like the way he felt himself.

'Were you going without me?'

'Of course not. But I was worried what you would think about Dermott telling me, I don't think you believe in Dermott any more than Dr Murgatroyd or my Mum does.' He was very offended and hurt, you could see it in his face and in the way he attacked the shoe leather, flicking at the laces which got in the way of the blue velvet pad with which he always put on the final shine.

'I do. Honestly.' Well then, that was all right. Kev relaxed somewhat but still felt angry.

'Matron is a cow. A cow. A cow.'

'Matron is a bitch, she was horrid to Magdalen. When she was the Queen, Matron used to laugh and hit her.'

'We can be Magdalen's protectors when we get outside. She needs somebody who understands, to protect her from those who don't.' It was a beautiful idea. They smilingly thought about it in silence for a while, and then the tea bell rang.

'I don't want any tea do you?' Kev nodded. So they went along for tea. During tea neither of them spoke. It was agreed behaviour between them, just in case nosy parkers were about. They even had a series of codes for 'pass the sugar' and 'do you want another cake'. You couldn't be too careful, people here reported things to the nurses.

They returned to their bedsides and Kev went on with the polishing.

'Kev, you've polished them already.'

'I know that but there's dust settling out of the air all the time.'

'Oh.' Toddy watched, as he always did, taking a vicarious pleasure in the brilliant shine. The black shoes had dancing taps underneath, little rattling metal plates. Kev had used to go in for tap dancing, he had won a marathon once, he had danced for hundreds of hours until they took him to hospital. He had won a lot of money but they hadn't given it to him, it had been for charity all the time and they hadn't told him. He had never danced again but he would like to. Magdalen had told him he should dance just for the pleasure of it, but Kev had said that he was inventing a new dance in his head and until he had decided what it was to be he wouldn't dance. Before that competition he had danced every day, but it was a long time ago. There was a picture of Fred Astaire over Kev's locker. Toddy sighed, wondering if there was anything good on television. He was glad he wasn't going home after all, because he had felt quite sure that *this* time he really was going to chop his mother up into bits. He'd had special orders to do that for as long as he could recall but hadn't dared to yet. He didn't really want to, he felt sure he would get caught, he always did whatever it was he'd done. But usually by his mother. Anyway, he could put if off again. They would go together and look for Magdalen instead. He looked forward to the trip very much. It would be the first time he'd been anywhere else besides either here or at home.

Maybe Magdalen would let him be the gardener at her house. She had a big garden and did almost all of it herself.

He made pictures in his mind about that.

Mowing the lawn. Weeding flowerbeds. Cutting a bunch of roses.

And then somehow the daydream went wrong, with lots of rain and somebody screaming. Did that mean anything?

It all had the feeling of something not quite right.

But he wouldn't mention it to Kev because he got cross about his premonitions. Mostly they never came to anything anyway, it had used to mean a fit coming on before the pills. Well, when he got out, he didn't intend taking the pills any more. He preferred the things that happened in his head after a fit, it wasn't awful at all. He looked forward to that too; life, thought Toddy, was full of promise.

37

Abel Murgatroyd was beginning the book, the first of a series, which would entirely change the face of modern psychiatry. Laing might have thought he'd done that but they hadn't seen anything yet. He put a sheet of blue copy paper down, then a sheet of carbon paper, then a white bank sheet, then another carbon, then a better quality top copy. He had been doing that for about half an hour and he found it calmed his mind. Blue, green, white, green, white, blue, and so on. Each sheet immaculate and the back of the carbon unmarked.

He had a new portable typewriter with a new black ribbon, a fine ballpoint and a bottle of correction fluid.

His task was not easy. He aimed to write a popular work which would be accessible to everyone, which would sell, and which would yet contain a great deal of very unusual material without seeming to be a crank book. Without being a crank book. This book must be revolutionary but not outrageous. People must be made to see that there were more things in heaven and earth, read about them without scoffing.

He needed a smash hit. More copies than *Games People Play* or *Sanity, Madness and the Family*. He would write nothing except the truth and try not to justify it too much – just reason where the facts seemed incredible.

He felt almost holy sitting there arranging paper for his work. He ran out of carbon paper so could stack no more sets. Well, it was time to begin. The material had dictated to him the beginning point – that was good, it was the environment speaking to him. Jung had worked like that a lot. It now seemed incredible that he should ever have doubted any of Jung's valuable ideas and reported experiences. But his mind had been closed, and now it was open.

He must not work too fast, but he must work every day. Even two hours would be something, you could probably write a lot in two hours. Perhaps it would be better to do a first draft and then sift the material? But yes, of course it would.

He should have known that – fancy thinking he could produce a great work straight off just like that. Lack of humility, that was a problem with him, always had been but he hadn't really seen it. Well, that needed cheaper paper. He hadn't any.

Abel Murgatroyd, author of a world shattering book on psychology, comparative religion, mystical experience and human behaviour, put on his jacket and set off to drive five miles into town to get a packet of cheap typewriting paper.

He could see why some famous writers had secretaries. This sort of thing wasted a lot of time, and he wanted to get *on* with it while the ideas were still fresh. Perhaps a small tape recorder was the answer? He parked near a shop with a display of sound equipment.

He spent two happy hours choosing a suitable machine, with the help of a very knowledgeable young person, and by the time he had purchased one, bought a plug, and got home, it was time to prepare dinner.

After dinner, he intended to begin trying out talking into the machine. He hoped he could not be heard through the thin walls of this temporary flat he had rented. Last night people had hammered on the walls just because he was meditating and doing his 'om' in the bathroom. It had sounded more resonant in there.

It was coming to something when people hammered on the walls of harmless hermits. That was precisely the kind of thing which would not happen when the world had read his book. People would understand. Everyone would be doing their 'om' in the bathroom by the time he had finished with them.

But first, how the devil did one cook dashi with ramen? He had bought it in a health food shop. The label was in Japanese – oh no – in English on the back. Seaweed, sesame, sunflower oil – it sounded marvellously good. Better than the steak and chips he had consumed so readily, poisoning his finer vibrations with animal substances. This was the food for hermits – plain vegetarian stuff. Someone knocked on the door. Damn. Sigh. Come in.

It was Miriam Goldsmith, his helper and acolyte.

'Miriam, I'm working.'

'Well you look as if you are cooking noodles to me, can I have some? I'm hungry.'

'OK. Sit down. Why did you come?'

'I'm depressed.'

'Good grief! I thought that was past.'

'Well yes, but this is actually about something.'

'Something?' How could anything intrude upon their happiness, now that they were working together upon this new work – or at least, he was, and she was helping.

'I'm not used to celibacy. I've never been celibate since I was thirteen.'

'Well it will do you good, I feel absolutely certain that my vision was correct, where the spirit of truth laid upon us a vow of celibacy during the making of the great work.'

Miriam didn't speak. She was beginning to be a bit pissed off with the whole thing. First Clive being no good then going to a psych then finding that this psych was crazy, even to the extent of thinking that Clive's dotty wife was a sort of Ark or something weird.

'Do you still dream about it?'

'Every night. I have a recurring dream about a black psych who turns out to be a magnificent fuck. He takes me dancing too.'

'Hm. Well never mind; here, have some ramen and dashi.'

'Some what?'

'Japanese noodles. Very good food.' Miriam gazed at the noodles and thought they looked like the threadworms her cat had once vomited up onto the top of the cooker at home. Her mother had also rushed off to vomit and found that she too had threadworms. The whole family had gone to the doctor and been given pills. Miriam laughed at the memory.

'I think it's going too far, that sort of thing is OK for nuns but I'm not a nun.'

'Yes you are – in a very special, new way.' Miriam sighed. The man was barmy really. She ate some noodles.

And yet, there was the problem she'd had about Clive's wife. That woman turning out to be Abel's patient, and everybody getting visions and dreams and so on – it was very weird.

'Let me help you with the book this evening then.'

'I've got a tape recorder, there's nothing on it yet. When I've got something, you can type it down as a first draft perhaps?'

'I hate typing. Let's have a look at the machine.' He indicated the tape recorder.

'Wow!' It was an excellent Japanese model with a great many knobs and switches. After a short while she had it in working order, and while Abel cleared the two soup dishes she sang off-the-cuff punk songs into the machine and played them back.

'When our New Movement gets started,
You soggy yobs is gonna turn your heads.
You gonna see the light dawning brightly
Like napalm in your wormy heads.

There was a hammering upon the wall. Abel lost his temper and hammered back with the dashi pan. The handle broke off. Miriam howled with laughter.

'Oh fuck it Miriam, that does it. Let's have a drink, come on.'

'Better than that. Let's have a drink and then go to bed. It'll inspire your work, not kill it.' She began opening a bottle of Muscadet that had stood in the fridge for several days. Abel froze, poised between two worlds. There were two ways to change the world. Through celibacy, temperance, meditation and vegetarianism. And the other way. Dionysian. Invoking the muse through the senses.

159

He watched in anguish as Miriam stripped off her clothes and then poured wine into two glasses. He did not speak as she found and opened a tin of corned beef and spread slices of it with mustard pickle.

'Come on sailor. Bed for us.' She took the tray of goodies over to his bedroom. He relaxed. Sighed.

Oh well, he would write the book tomorrow. This was precisely the sort of thing that Tolstoy must have had to put up with – and it hadn't stopped him in the end.

38

Clive set up his tent in the beach encampment at Asilah, having decided earlier that he did not much like the look of Casablanca, Bogart or no Bogart. It had been a long and tedious drive north to get here, and although it was not beautiful, it was all right from the point of view of swimming, beach, and camp facilities. He struggled with the guy ropes to get the erection he desired, then tied a washing line from the tent pole to a nearby fence. His next job was to do a bit of laundering.

The laundry turned out to be a stone slab beneath a tap but he was used by now to scrubbing things in cold water. Strangely, they came out clean – it must be soft water and the nature of the dirt which here was not industrial. A young man came to scrub at the next slab.

'They ought to have women to do this job didn't they?' said the man in an Australian whine. He had a mass of curly black hair and Jewish-looking features tanned dark.

'Yes, they did. At Mohamedia there were washerwomen, lovely little Berber girls with green tattoos.'

'I've lived with the Berbers. Those Berber women are ideal if you ask me. They get up at dawn to grind the meal and bake bread every day, they do the laundry then they clean the living quarters. They do pottery, make silverware, weave rugs and blankets, sell them, they really keep things together. And they aren't always nosing into the men's affairs either, they get on with their thing like having babies, they love babies.' He was scrubbing some tattered underpants. The jeans he wore, his only clothing, were patched and repatched with one brilliant scarlet piece on the seat.

'Where did you get the red patch? A Berber lady sew it on for you?'

'Nah. An English bird I met last time I was in England. I went to the Reading bash and she invited me back to her pad and mended all my clothes for me. Bright red is good luck.'

'Oh.' Clive thought perhaps he had birds everywhere who did things for him, lucky chap.

'I suppose you travel a lot. I'm just on holiday, on my way back now, to England as it happens.'

'Really? I'm heading for England, Reading bash again then Edinburgh, I've got some friends putting on a play there, thought I might drop by.'

'How nice. My name is Clive Hayward.' He extended a soapy hand. The man was going to say something but stopped and told him instead that his name was Mark Kleiman. Clive had not done all his laundry so Mark picked up a shirt from Clive's pile and began pounding it on the slab. Clive watched with dismay as he saw his raw silk shirt being scrubbed up into linty balls. But if people offered to help you it was very difficult to prevent them.

'When you leaving?' Mark asked, pounding away as heavily as any Berber washerwoman.

'Day after tomorrow possibly.'

'Oh great, then maybe we can go out together tonight. I know a great caff where they do a cheap couscous. I know some of the Arabs here. Not women of course, all blokes in the café, they talk together, women at home.'

'That's one good thing about places like Morocco, one does at least know which sex one is.'

'Right.'

Clive indulged in the feeling of all being right with the world; women cooked and bore children – and did laundry – men talked over world affairs and philosophy together. One didn't respect oneself doing too many menial tasks, it took away human dignity.

'Let's go for some beer first,' said Clive, meaning a bottle of nasty Arab beer rather than a foaming tankard but Mark was disgusted with that idea.

'Nah. Never touch alcohol, the vibes are too low. But we could go for a smoke if you like.' Clive didn't like that idea, he'd never smoked and thought it dangerous. He was not of the drug generation.

'I don't smoke, never tried it.'

'Well maybe you should. It's in my family not to drink, my father was against it – back in Melbourne that is you know, very unusual but Jews are moderate you see, peace loving.'

'Yes. The middle way,' Clive heard himself say fatuously.

'But I'd never go back to Australia. Couldn't even if I wanted to, they'd put me in jail.'

'Good Lord. Why?'

'Drugs, and freaking out when a copper hit me.'

'What happened?' Clive felt uncomfortable.

'Well, for no good reason this fuzz hit me and I saw red, I pushed him away, he smacked me in the mouth I hit him in the balls and ran. They didn't catch me but I know they know who it was, somebody grassed.' Clive felt indignation on Mark's behalf in spite of some nagging doubt that the story was not accurate.

'My mother doesn't want me back, doesn't want the shame of her son in jail. Suits me, don't like Australia.'

'I see.'

'I think I'm an Arab at heart anyway, they're both Semitic peoples you know, and I get on real well with the Arabs in Morocco, and the Berbers although they aren't Arabs they feel like Arabs to me. It should all be the same anyway.'

They went to hang out their laundry and then for showers. Mark displayed some nasty-looking sores in his groin.

'Man, you ever see anything like these, is it the pox or what?'

'I've never seen the pox. You should go to a doctor.' Clive almost ran out of the washroom in horror.

'You're joking, no doctors for me. They give you those antibiotic things, I prefer natural cures, herbs and stuff.'

'Herbs can't cure the pox otherwise the Middle Ages

wouldn't have been riddled with it.'

'It might not be the pox. But it worries me. I'd hate to lose the use of my old man. I'd commit suicide if that happened.' Did one lose the use . . .? Clive was scared.

'Have you been with any dubious women?'

'All women are dubious.'

Clive laughed, told himself not to be silly, you couldn't catch syphilis just through being in the same shower room. Could you? He would have a check at a special clinic when he got back to England, just in case. Microscopes and antibiotics were useful weapons; he believed in them.

Later, when they arrived at Mark's favourite Arab café, Clive demurred. It was obviously filthy and he dare not take so great a risk of dysentery. Mark in his eager whine said he had eaten there scores of times and never had any bad results.

'You are probably immune by now, living rough. I've got very sensitive bowels. Tell you what, if you come to a cleaner place, I'll stand you a meal.' There was no denying that as well as grateful acquiescence there was triumph in Mark's face. He lived by conning and he had conned again; the life force manifesting is a joyful thing thought Clive ironically.

They chose an Arab-French place which turned out to be run by an English ex-army type. Perhaps he had stayed in North Africa after the war, or perhaps he had been here even before Bogart? There was much to-do about the menu, Mark preferred wholefoods but the meal when it finally got chosen and served was excellent. They had chicken Marocain which had tadjin spice, sesame seeds and raisins; saffron rice, tiny green beans and green salad which looked unreal, the first green stuff Clive had seen in the hot Moroccan climate. Imported, accounting for its high price. They also had Arab pastries full of honey and nuts and a mediocre white wine which was at least chilled. The coffee was excellent and Clive had brandy. They relaxed, glowing with repletion. Clive would have preferred less chatter but Mark had kept up a flow all through the meal.

He told all the wonders and joys of being a traveller and Clive was paying attention but became aware of a distancing from the words. There was a buzzing in his ears and his fingers and toes felt strange. Clive began to feel faint, so bent down to pretend to tie his shoelace, hoping the flow of blood to his head would clear the feeling. It did not. He sat up. Everything in the room seemed very far away. His body was making signals to him, and with a great effort he got up and went as fast as he could to the men's room, only just in time to vomit violently into the bowl. He couldn't believe it. Then he had a violent attack of the shits, then more vomiting, sweat pouring off him all over. What the devil . . .? He threw up again, gazed at his wavering image in the mirror over the basin, and his knees gave way bringing him to unconsciousness on the tiled floor. When he came to he felt much better and was able to rise and wash his face and comb his hair. How ghastly, how stupid. Food poisoning, must be. Good God.

Back at the table Mark laughed.

'You'd have been better off at the other place maybe.'

Clive felt too weak to argue and also strangely euphoric. They strolled back to the camp in a very friendly way, gazing at the moon, feeling the soft night air, and Clive's experience seemed to have done him no harm. He felt fine, he did not even mind having paid a very large bill and been made sick. He felt like smiling at everyone they passed, and everyone smiled back. He felt very tired. After a weak attempt at thanks, Mark left him at his tent. Clive got straight into his sleeping bag and slept immediately.

His dream was the most vivid he had ever had; the colours were so bright that he afterwards recalled them, not a usual feature of his dreaming. The sequence of events was not dreamlike, and it was not until he woke up that he could have for a moment known he was dreaming, had he thought to compare the two states. In the collecting heat of the morning sun, Clive recalled his dream.

He had got up and walked once more into the town, but not a part that Mark had shown him. He had gone to an apothecary as if directed, having no hesitation at which turns to take. He had found it occupied by an old man, and requested of him in

English a suitable preparation for the cure of venereal ulcers. Without speaking, the man had ground and mixed herbs and seeds, mixed it with liquids from two jars and put it into an empty Coke bottle. By signs he had indicated that two small spoonsful were to be taken on rising and on retiring. Clive had paid rather a large number of dirhams for this stuff and departed with a handshake. He had walked all the way back to the campsite and gone back to sleep.

He pondered on this dream before getting up, wondering with a sort of secret shame if there might be something in it; if perhaps it was after all possible for the unconscious mind to know things of value, to transmit them through dreams. But no, that could hardly be it; he had simply rehashed the events of the day, recalling Mark's comment that herbs would cure his sores better than antibiotics. He sprang up, impatient with his betrayal of his rational mind and knocked over the Coke bottle which was by the door of his tent. Fortunately the top was secure. Good God!

His impulse was to run to Mark with the medicine but also to throw the stuff away – doubtless he had noticed the Coke bottle before sleeping, and it had caused his dream! There was always an explanation. But when he put on his clothes he could not help looking through his wallet. He knew exactly how much money he had after the dinner, he had checked to know if he should go to the bank the following day. He had decided that he would have sufficient, but now he would not. He had paid fifty dirhams for the mixture, and he was that much short. What the hell was going on? Mark's shadow fell across his thoughts.

'Hi! Fantastic day!'

'You're telling me. I don't suppose actually that you will be as inclined to disbelieve what I'm just going to tell you as I do myself.' Mark sat down, grinning, expectant, his eyes flickering across the contents of Clive's wallet.

Feeling a fool, Clive recounted his night.

'Wow! I guess this looks like a real psychic experience. Here, let's have a sniff at the bottle. Mark sniffed, so did Clive. A strong herbal odour, not really unpleasant. Mark shook it gently and asked for a spoon.

'You must be mad, you might get poisoned.'

'I don't think so. I think this stuff will cure me, I've heard of this kind of thing before. Man, you know what? You got out of your body last night and got me this stuff back from the spirit world. Sorcerers do that kind of thing regularly. And also, I've got a confession to make.' Clive frowned as he watched Mark swallow his medicine.

'It's quite nice, bit like cough mixture but more bitter. Yeah, well, I doped your food last night. Don't be angry, I guess that's what made you sick but that sometimes happens at first. You must have had enough to project you.'

Clive was furious, but not really with Mark. He had heard so much of that kind of thing from Magdalen he was pig sick of it, and now here was someone saying that it had happened to him! Projected – out of his body of course, into other worlds. Well, the world had been real – er – a dreamworld, it could be checked out. Without pausing for breakfast they set off together, Clive following his dream route to the apothecary's place. There was the house, but the man there was already beating brass vases, his furnace attended by a small boy with bellows.

'See, it isn't an apothecary's place. Just a dream.'

'Hey man,' Mark addressed the metal-worker. 'You been here long?' The man knew a little French and English. Between the three of them they established that it had been a metal-worker's shop for fifteen years, before that a bakery, and before that a herbalist, a man specialising in sorcery.

Mark was dancing with triumph, his dirty bare feet whirling up the dust.

'Man oh man, are you a head, a natural!' But Clive did not want to discuss the matter any more. He wanted his breakfast, to get out of this town, to head for home. He was easily persuaded to take Mark along, he felt too disturbed and preoccupied to argue.

'But for god's sake don't put any more dope into my food. I don't want it, and I mean that.'

'OK, OK. I'm sorry, I maybe shouldn't have – but you must

admit it got results.'

'I admit nothing of the kind, there must be a rational explanation. And I wouldn't drink that stuff for anything.

'Well, it wasn't meant for you, I'll take it and we'll see the cure. Thanks very much indeed by the way.' Fifty dirhams were lost, but of course, a note could have fallen from his pocket, it was easy to have money stolen too.

He would advise Mark very strongly to go to a specialist clinic and not depend upon the dubious contents of the Coke bottle. He would go himself, just in case. Sometimes he felt as if Magdalen's craziness was like a virus; she believed herself to have supernatural experiences, or something of the sort, and he as a pragmatist did not believe in such things. And yet here he was almost subscribing to the paranoia of a pothead, almost mixing up dream and reality. He would get some high potency vitamin B complex the moment he got to a reliable health food shop, his nerves were not all they could be. Teaching was very draining. Everything was very draining.

'Do you ever feel you've been here before?' Mark said suddenly, as they were looking for somewhere to park in Fez.

'Sometimes. It is an electrical fault in the brain.'

Mark ignored that and went on, 'I do. Especially here in Morocco. I have this feeling you know as if I'd been a wealthy and important man with lots of wives once. I got it particularly strong last time I went through here. I felt as if I'd lost something really amazing.' He was silent for a short while. 'You know, as if I'd done something wrong and it needed to be put right.'

'I'm afraid I don't believe in reincarnation. Statistics are against its credibility.'

'Statistics! Hell man, you can prove or disprove *anything* with statistics. They don't mean a damn thing.'

39

The grey capsule around her, the voice of the alien, they were there, but as Magdalen awoke she felt differently about them. She felt at ease within herself, full of confidence. The voice was communicating.

'We shall not be bringing you a male companion. We regret to say we find their vibrations unsuitable for you at present.' She smiled. She didn't need them to tell her that and furthermore, that was fine with her!

'We are contemplating sending you back to earth in the near future.' About time.

'Good. I have things to do. But this isn't the last of our contacts, is it?' She would miss them.

'No. You may return. What is your wish for breakfast?' What could they mean by 'may'? That she would possibly return? That it was permissible to return? She thought it wiser not to get into a linguistics snarl-up before breakfast, which, she told them, would need to be substantial, she was starving. Oatmeal, kippers, wholemeal bread and unsalted butter, coarse marmalade, coffee, fresh fruit and figs, the whole bit. Yum. There was no response to her order so she opened her eyes.

She saw her little travelling clock on the beside cabinet, she had fifteen minutes to get ready or she would miss breakfast altogether at this small Northumberland hotel. The room was clean but ugly, the view from the window stunning as she pulled back the brocade curtains; beautiful moorland on rolling hills. She had a longish drive, the earlier the start the better. Rather boring, that reality.

She showered hastily in the closet down the hall, allowing the water to help wash away her negative thoughts – no life was boring, it was not that. Life was a problem to be solved, in the sense of what to do next. Several decisions would have to be made, some of them mutual decisions with Clive, over property and so on. Perhaps it could be best managed through a solicitor? After all, that was one of their functions, go-between. A female solicitor, somebody who knew how to handle things properly. But she had to go back to White House to get some things she needed. If he was there, she didn't want verbal aggression. Well, take things one at a time, wait and see. If he started in with the sophistry, the red herrings across her thought and – dammit woman, she told herself, stop worrying! Today, and henceforth, you are equal to anything! Maybe.

The breakfast was wonderful, exactly what she had hoped for, the bread was home-made. She was the only guest, the place was like a morgue. Just right for rising from!

Very glad to finally be on her way, the car behaving well, she selected further inspiration in the form of Deep Purple playing 'Smoke on the Water' at full blast. Singing along, foot down, she sped from the beautiful scenery towards the scruffy Midlands.

Would the magnolia still be in bloom?

Suddenly she was coasting on the M6, the engine had cut out. Some garage that had been! She drifted over on to the hard shoulder, knowing already that she was as far from an RAC telephone as was possible. Perhaps it was damp on the leads, or something had become detached? She got out into the slipstream of passing vehicles and investigated under the bonnet. Everything seemed to be in place. Heck.

'We are very sorry to impede you like this, it seems to be an effect we cannot avoid causing.' Ah! What now? She could see nothing untoward. Surely they were not going to take her away again? Magdalen felt no fear, just curiosity.

'What do you want now?'

'We forgot to warn you. We think it would be better for you if you told nothing about us. From our data we surmise that you will not be believed.'

'But I have told one or two people, I think – yes of course I did. I was thought crazy.'

'Precisely. Perhaps you did not need this warning?'

'I don't know. On the whole I agree with you. Maybe someday I will find someone I could trust.'

'Consult us first.' Two cars almost collided as their engines cut out, and then a juggernaut went silent; the hard shoulder was becoming crowded.

'Thanks for the reminder anyway. But actually I don't know how to get in touch with you. I don't suppose for one moment that you are in the phone book.'

'No. What is that?' She grinned at their lack of knowledge in some directions, but of course, they would find a telephone quaint.

'It's one of our communication devices. I was joking.'

'Oh. Joke. We shall investigate this phone book.'

'The book isn't the device, it is a kind of catalogue.'

'Sex again. Nearly everything with humans is to do with sex, is this not so?'

'You could say that. It does seem to get into everything sooner or later.'

'Just call us the way you always do.' What? There was a crackling sound of static in her hair, an uprush of musical sound and a gust of hot wind. The driver of the car in front came running towards her looking crazed.

'My God did you see that? Did you see that?'

'What are we looking at?' enquired Magdalen, very cool.

'A–a, it was – a flying saucer!'

'Well no I didn't. What did it look like?'

'It – well – light – it – it . . .'

She smiled. 'Try a bit of deep breathing. You must be overtired.'

And she got in the car, started it without trouble, and simply drove away. She had more immediate things to do than get mixed up in that. Such as, how would she earn her living? She painted, but it would not keep her. She had been largely a dependent wife. She changed the Deep Purple and put on a spooky Miles Davis but after a few miles it began to bring her down so she chanced Janis Joplin. Guts. Yes indeed. Something would turn up, she had all kinds of skills. She could have been an actress, she could be anything.

Her heart beat faster as she approached the avenue where White House stood. She parked in the next street, not quite admitting to herself that she was snooping to see if Clive were around. Did she want to see him? She had not come for a confrontation. He might be out.

She sweated somewhat, approaching their house, slipping in fallen lilac slimy after rain, noting with distaste that the council had put tarmac over the lovely old paving stones. She had loved them, uneven, mossy, and no more dangerous than this stuff which gripped blossom and leaf. The front wall of the garden leaned outwards, possibly in need of urgent rebuilding. She envisioned inevitable decay, the eventual death of this beautiful house in some time which felt like now. But there it was whole and not even in need of painting; it would fetch a packet. Half of it was hers. It had been too large for the two of them. Sell it. He could adapt, as she was adapting. Adapt or die, she felt this in herself.

Still she shrank from walking right in, and found her approach furtive, taking care not to disturb the noisy gravel, and, in the porch, carefully trying the door to find it open. She did not enter yet, but warily turned to walk up the side path which led through the fruit garden into the large back garden. Her eye noticed the black branches of the magnolia as she turned, but she restrained herself from gazing upwards into it, her instinct made her preserve herself from further intimacy with that tree, which was the tree of Clive and Magdalen. She heard voices.

'Well, I'd start a new compost heap over there Kev if I was you but try not to get your wellies muddy because you'll be washing them again and you do more wellie-washing than weeding. And I'll prune the gooseberries but keep the clippings separate from the weeds because they wunna rot.' What the devil was going on? Two gardeners? Clive must be barmy, they could not afford that kind of help. Magdalen felt indignation, and also a great deal of curiosity coupled with the certainty that she must not show herself. She edged along by clipped beeches where she could gain a view of the conservatory through which there was access to the back garden. It was occupied.

There was a young and very Jewish man tampering with the grapevine, and sitting in Magdalen's cane lounger a beautiful girl who looked vaguely familiar, her platinum hair striped with one perfect violet stripe. She was reading aloud from a book but Magdalen was not near enough to hear. The cover bore a Sufi symbol, it was probably one of her Idris Shah collections.

Angry and feeling dispossessed she wondered if perhaps she should go away and telephone first? It was irritating not being able to go around the back of the house to explore. She looked harder at the girl and recalled having met her in a department store. She was a student of Clive's whom she had been introduced to once at a staff-student bash, Miriam something, somebody's wealthy daughter. Magdalen decided to risk going in the house. After all, it was her own house!

There were voices from the kitchen and dining room, so she went straight upstairs but stopped short at a sudden blast of music from the drawing room. Heavy dub reggae, how very uncharacteristic. It reminded her of Royston and caused a sudden sexual lurch of such violence that she clutched herself. Long moments later she took hold of her feelings and with a deep breath sighed outwards as she continued upstairs.

'Remember, you invented that guy. A nonesuch!' It was not much consolation, but it was sobering. She entered the master bedroom cautiously.

It was as she gazed at the obvious signs of a double bed slept in by two people that a clanging gong sounded loudly. In response to this sound there were banging doors, the reggae ceased, feet rushed. It seemed that several people were going out into the back garden. She hurried away from the bedroom and saw below her in the hall a large pile of mail where hers was always put, ostentatiously unread – until after she had first opened them. Upon investigating she found three from friends abroad, including one from Louis Sakoian whom she had not seen for ten years or more. How extraordinary! She read it avidly. He had been cleaning out his attic in his New Jersey house and found her letters, mouse-nibbled, had read them and cursed himself for letting go of the friendship. He was now divorced and would dearly love to open a correspondence, maybe even see her again some day. She stood for a while, pondering. It was a fortuitous time for such a letter to arrive. A trip to the States might be just the opening she needed. Had he changed? Divorced – he hadn't been married when she had known him. How the web of relationships opened and closed, knotted and crossed, plaited and parted. To go rushing off and have an affair in America – did it not look like fate at work?

Fate or not, she crumpled the letter and went and burned it in the empty drawing room waste paper bin. Sorry Louis, but no. I'm on my own planet, out to lunch, and I like it by myself. She poked the ashes until they dispersed, dead.

She went right to the top of the house to the attic with the dormer window overlooking the back garden. From here she could see what was happening.

The window catch was rusty but with firmness she got it open only to find that it hung on one fragile hinge and could fall three storeys. It was heavy, but she held it level and open, extremely tense as she observed below her a most extraordinary scene.

There were about twenty people standing around in either leotards or karate pyjamas, taking instruction from a dimly recognisable Abel Murgatroyd. His hair was longer and he wore beads and purple ankle warmers with his leotard.

'. . . and then you visualise a vivid blue circle just below your breast bone. You are getting smaller and smaller, and travelling in towards this circle . . .' Magdalen's jaw fell open and she almost relaxed her hold on the window, for there was Clive, dressed in his old fencing costume with a saffron sash tied around the waist, obeying Abel along with the rest. Two of the chaps had been gardeners at Twelve Trees. There were three sets of mature dreadlocks, an unlikely sight in a yoga class, if that was what it was. There was so much hair she could not detect if one of them was Royston from where she stood, arm trembling.

'And I feel her coming close to us, our Magdalen will be with us, to guide us.' She had heard correctly.

'We must be prepared for Her. We must keep in constant touch with our Higher Centres, keep our channels pure, and be fitted to greet Her when she comes to us. The Anaharata Chakra is our. . .' She had heard the capital letter and in a flash saw what was going on. Her reaction was acute embarrassment and a sense of urgency. She must get out quick.

It was with difficulty that she managed to fasten the window in silence, and then she moved fast, filling two cases with her paints and brushes, useful clothes and her best winter boots. If there was one thing she could not stand it was yoga classes, she found disco dancing much more beneficial for both body and spirit. And as for being turned into a guru, that was *out*. What on earth were they thinking of? How exactly did she feature in their imaginations? Clive and Doc Murgatroyd – oh, get away, get away, she needed no explanation, it must be an example of group hysteria or something of the sort. Blue circles! The guy was nuts!

She snatched a cameo brooch that Clive had given her, and then dropped it back on to the dusty dressing table. She needed no souvenirs. She called a cab from the bedside extension and got all her things out on to the front path as it arrived.

'It's only in the next street but I can't manage all this stuff.'

'It'll cost you the first pound, Madam.'

'It'd be worth a hundred pounds to get away from here, just hurry up, would you.' The driver smiled full of irony, and did as he was asked.

JEN GREEN & SARAH LEFANU,
Editors
DESPATCHES FROM THE FRONTIERS
OF THE FEMALE MIND
An Anthology of Original Stories

A collection of startling new science fiction stories from
well-known authors, including Zoë Fairbairns, Mary Gentle,
Gwyneth Jones, Tanith Lee, Naomi Mitchison, Joanna Russ,
Josephine Saxton, Alice Sheldon, Lisa Tuttle, Pamela Zoline;
and introducing new writers Lannah Battley, Penny Casdagli,
Margaret Elphinstone, Frances Gapper, Beverley Ireland,
Pearlie McNeill, Sue Thomason.

This collection comes from the frontiers and offers a glimpse
of what lies beyond.

sf

0 7043 3973 0
£2.50

JOANNA RUSS
EXTRA(ORDINARY) PEOPLE

Five elegant stories from Hugo and Nebula award-winning author Joanna Russ, in the form of a history lesson to a child of the future. A mediaeval abbess defends her community against Viking invasion; a young girl sails on a 19th-century clipper with a guardian who is not what 'he' seems; a future utopia fails to satisfy the desires of arrivals from the twentieth century; a time traveller disguises herself as an arch-demon in primitive Ruritania; an author evolves the plot of a Gothic romance between two women.

Joanna Russ once more draws on her talent for vivid characterisation to involve us in worlds not our own, exploring gender and power relationships in past and future to illuminate our own time.

Extra(Ordinary) People 'retells history for a girl of the future, with wit and pity' *Guardian*

'Solidly visualised, verbally precise' *New Statesman*

'*Extra(Ordinary) People* reinforces Russ's reputation as one of the ablest and most stylish writers working in science fiction' *City Limits*

sf

0 7043 3950 1
£1.95

JOANNA RUSS
THE FEMALE MAN

'A visionary novel about a society where women can do all
we now fantasize in closets and kitchens and beds ...
intricate, witty, furious, savage' Marge Piercy

'A sophisticated work' *Sunday Times*

'A book women can read with glee' *City Limits*

The Female Man extends the boundaries of science fiction. It
explores language and sexuality, customs and conventions,
dreams and nightmares. It provides a witty and subversive
analysis of the power men hold over women in our society.

0 7043 3949 8   £1.95

THE ADVENTURES OF ALYX

Alyx – assassin, thief, hired bodyguard
Alyx – courageous, cunning and loyal to her own interests
Alyx – professional picklock, dragonslayer and wit
Alyx – 'among the wisest of a sex that is surpassingly wise'

The Adventures of Alyx are witty, serious, entertaining and
profound. Alyx is a heroine beyond our wildest dreams.

0 7043 3972 2   £1.95

sf

SUZETTE HADEN ELGIN
NATIVE TONGUE

The year is 2179. Contact with other worlds has been established, and Earth has begun its colonisation of the stars. The arrival of ambassadors from outer space is an everyday occurrence, but communication with them is still a problem.

The dynasties of the Linguists have taken on the task of talking to the aliens, and immense power has fallen into their hands – into the hands of their men, that is. For here as in every aspect of society, the male reigns supreme – legislation has crushed the women's movement and women are barred from holding public office, they are minors in the eyes of the law.

This is a novel of the cold war between the sexes, of the hidden resistance of the women Linguists who develop Láadan, a secret language of their own. Suzette Haden Elgin, science fiction author and professor of linguistics, combines her talents to create a society in which interplanetary trade has made language study a valuable commodity – and thereby handed the so-called 'weaker sex' a weapon for liberation . . . if they dare to use it.

0 7043 3971 4
£2.50

MARGE PIERCY
WOMAN ON THE EDGE OF TIME

Connie Ramos is thirty-seven, Mexican–American, worn-out, labelled, discarded by a society which has declared her insane and taken away first her lover, then her child, finally her own freedom.

As the drugged, helpless inmate of a public mental hospital, she is offered only one way back to the casually violent urban 'normality' from which she was snatched: participation in a mind-control experiment using electronic implantations in the brain.

But Connie is also a 'catcher' – able to visit and take part in a translucent future of ecological and social harmony. In it sex roles are unknown, biological relationships have given way to a broader concept of family, and the likenesses of her lost child and lover live on in a rare atmosphere of liberty and possibility. As the doctors close in, this poignant vision becomes a vivid counterpoint to the intensifying horror of Connie's reality. But gradually she comes to seize her own power to act – not only for herself but also for the future.

0 7043 3837 8
£3.50